A NIGHT AT THE INNS AND OTHER STORIES

By the same author:

Brief Cases

An Eye on the Whiplash and Other Stories

A Night at the Inns
and Other Stories

HENRY MURPHY

BLACKHALL
Publishing

Blackhall Publishing
Lonsdale House
Avoca Avenue
Blackrock
Co. Dublin
Ireland

e-mail: info@blackhallpublishing.com
www.blackhallpublishing.com

ISBN: 978-1-84218-170-6 (HBK)
978-1-84218-145-4 (PBK)

A catalogue record for this book is available from the British Library.

Printed in Ireland by ColourBooks Ltd.

for

Colin, Jenny, Stephen, Declan, Eoghan and Cillian.

Henry Murphy is a barrister. His previous collections of short stories about Dermot McNamara, *An Eye on the Whiplash and Other Stories* (1997) and *Brief Cases* (2000), were published by Ashfield Press. *Brief Cases* is also available as an audio book, narrated by Des Keogh.

ACKNOWLEDGEMENTS

I would like to thank:

Elizabeth Brennan for her excellent and tactful editing;

Gerard O'Connor and Blackhall Publishing for continuing to publish my ravings;

Martyn Turner for illuminating the cover and our lives over the years;

Mary, Frank Murphy, Francis D. Murphy, Jack FitzGerald and Conor Bowman for reading the text – they say they did – encouraging and advising.

Henry Murphy
October 2008

CONTENTS

FIRST DAY BACK

*The Benchers of the Honorable Society of King's Inns
request the pleasure of the presence of
Dermot McNamara, B.L.
at morning coffee
in
King's Inns, Henrietta Street,
on Monday the 4th day of October, at 11.00 a.m.,
on the occasion of the commencement of
the Michaelmas Law Term.*

I had been dreading this invitation ever since its predecessor dropped through the letterbox a year before. Its
arrival marked the ending of the 'long vacation', the two
words – after 'brief fee' – closest to the hearts of all
barristers.

The long vacation begins each year on 31 July, unless
of course this date falls on a Saturday or Sunday, in
which happy circumstance it begins the previous Friday.
On that day, the courts close down until October. There is
a sense of finishing school for the summer: 'No more Irish,
no more French, no more sitting on the hard old bench ...'
The legal diary that tells of pending cases is half full at
best, and our individual diaries have 'LONG VACATION'
scratched in big bold print across the pages of August and
September. On that day, the first Monday in October
seems aeons away.

It takes a number of years for a barrister to develop the appropriate strategy for the long vacation. For example, some barristers like to stay behind for a week or two to work on the backlog of paperwork that has accumulated in the countdown to the holiday period. Others have found from bitter experience that the eyelids insist on closing and that, no matter how hard one tries to keep them open, any attempt at paperwork at the beginning of August is in vain.

Rachel and I have come to the conclusion that the most efficient way of approaching the long vacation is to get away immediately with the twins, Kate and Conor, for a week or two to Donegal, usually a week for Rachel and two for me. Invariably, an urgent consultation cuts short Rachel's holiday, an eventuality that she insists causes her great disappointment. During these two weeks by the Atlantic it is easy to believe that the Law Library does not exist and that there is no necessity to earn a living. Unfortunately, the days when barristers lived on, rather than in, estates have long since gone and, for most, it is necessary to earn a crust. Come the second half of August, it is difficult to deny the falling leaves and chestnuts of autumn.

September, in a way, is a lie. We all know we are well and truly in the second half of the vacation, but we resist it. Some by golf, some by fishing in Connemara, others by flight. We all do our best to keep the truth at bay, but, inevitably, time and the long vacation pass and not even an injunction will prevent Postman Pat from popping the unsolicited invitation through the letterbox.

There are few issues upon which the Bar is united and fewer upon which it is as passionately united as the necessity to cling to the long vacation. Ian Paisley does not hold on to the Union Jack as zealously. It is part of what a barrister is. In constitutional terms the long vacation is an inalienable right. There must be no dilution, no surrender.

Unfortunately, one way or another, the first Monday in October tends to turn up, usually in rain. Rachel and I rarely travel to work together but we make an exception for the first day of term. Setting foot inside the Four Courts after the interlude is like returning to school after the summer holidays. It takes a few days to forget sand and sea, to get used to wearing a suit again and to remember the names of colleagues not thought about since July.

Neither of us are of a spiritual disposition but, nonetheless, if only out of superstition, we like to attend the annual Mass to which we have been invited. Who knows what professional ill might befall us in the year ahead were we to miss this opportunity to pay homage to our spiritual judge? The religious world may be experiencing a downturn in vocations, but there is no shortage of forensic altar boys for the annual Mass. Male members of the Bar, whose theology is unlikely to be over-influenced by Vatican II, pack the altar, while their leader shakes the thurible with gusto, in celebration of the good old days. Meanwhile, our separated brethren gather separately in other city centre retreats.

The sermon is given by a lightly left-of-centre auxiliary bishop who, were it not for the influence of the cast assembled on the altar, might be fully fledged. On account of the fact that the auxiliary has little familiarity with the day-to-day workings of the legal system, his sermon tends to be somewhat naïve. Judges are exhorted to treat witnesses with courtesy and respect, to decide cases on the evidence and to eschew prejudice. On the other hand, barristers are urged to prepare properly, to give time to their clients and, above all, to turn up. The sermon goes above the heads of the congregation and, as soon as Saint Dominic's school choir brings the ceremony to an end with its final beautiful hymn, we are all off to tea and buns in King's Inns.

Even now my mother believes that this invitation to morning coffee represents overdue recognition of my progress as a Junior Counsel on the part of the alumni of the profession. She is not aware that every practising barrister is invited. Anxious to hold on to any morsel of esteem in which she still holds me, I do nothing to disabuse her of this harmless notion.

Traditionally, the tea and buns all but run out as soon as the elderly benchers who manage the institution have been helped to them, so you have to resort to holiday chat and tips for the judicial vacancies. Most present need little prompting to discuss at length the various holiday horizons they sailed or flew to and the volume of post that awaited them on their return. If you are alert you might even see the chance to slip off and swipe the last biscuit without your absence being noted. Needless to say, just as you are about to share your own riveting adventure with them, they spot someone to whom they must speak as a matter of some urgency. All the while, the proceedings are overlooked by a host of former chief justices who, in their day, enjoyed the occasion more than their portraits give them credit for.

There was absolutely no point in attempting to extricate Rachel from the circle of admiring Senior Counsel and judges of which she was the centre. In the company of Mark, friend and confidant, I made my way through the fish and fruit markets and back to the Library. I resolved, as I do every year, that next year I would forego the buns in the Inns and instead concentrate on the pursuit of money and justice from the outset.

'Anything on today?' I asked Mark as we entered the judges' yard, an area where their cars and not the judges themselves are kept.

'No, Dermot. Thankfully. What about you?'

'Me neither, which is precisely how I like it for the first few days at least.' I could hardly believe my ears. Was it really me saying that? It wasn't long since I would have welcomed a brief for Christmas Day if the court would sit. Here I was hoping for a gentle introduction to the new term, preferring gradual ingratiation with the grey, stony sea to the instant immersion favoured by so many barristers. Coffee seemed like a good idea.

'I just want to put my wig and gown into my locker and then I'll join you. Can you get me that new stuff, the Rombutts please,' I said. There was no question of me giving the coffee its correct pronunciation. To call it 'Rombouts' might suggest you were getting above yourself or were interested in a chancery practice.

I was shaking some summer cobwebs off my wig and gown and sharing a commencement-of-term pleasantry with a colleague, when I heard my name called. 'Dermot McNamara!' There was certainly nothing wrong with Tommy's voice after the break.

As I made my way up from the intestines of the Four Courts, I hoped that this summons would not interfere with my date with Mark. After all, we had a lot to catch up on. He had taken to the golf courses of the Algarve for the last week of the vacation to prepare himself mentally for the rigours of the new term and we had to discuss the in-the-meantime happenings.

'Good morning, Tommy.'

'Good morning, sir.'

Tommy, our much cherished receptionist, was many years my senior and, no matter how many times I asked him to call me by my Christian name, he refused to do so. 'I know that's the fashion nowadays, sir, the modern way as you might say,' Tommy had explained to me several times over as many pints, 'but I'm of the old school. "Sir" or "Mr" is what I was taught by my predecessor and I'm too old to change now.' I had given up.

'Did you have a good vacation, sir?' Tommy asked.

'I did indeed, thank you. And how about you?'

'Frankly, I'm glad to be back. Too much time on my hands. Missed the hustle and bustle.'

I surveyed the Square Hall, which was separated from the Library itself by Tommy's desk, to identify who was looking for me, but in vain. Not a soul I knew.

'Tommy, any idea who called me?' I asked.

'Yes. I did. I called you.' Tommy enjoyed this banter, drawing attention to my lack of precision. Thank God he wasn't a judge.

'Quite right. Bit rusty after the vacation. Who asked you to call me?'

'That's better, sir. You're in luck. A smasher, a real smasher. I'm sure I've seen her with you before, but if I have I can't put a name on her. Seemed a bit hassled. I told her that, as far as I was aware, you hadn't retired over the summer, but that I hadn't seen you yet this term. She went towards the restaurant.'

'Thanks, Tommy. If she comes back will you tell her I'm in?'

'Of course.'

I went in pursuit.

There are two restaurants. One is on the ground floor, which is for barristers only and in which Mark was now sitting with two Rombutts. The other is downstairs and is what might be called nowadays an inclusive restaurant, catering for the public. As I turned the corner at the top

6

of the stairs I was nearly knocked over by a young lady in a hurry. I didn't recognise her at first. When I last saw her in July her hair was as long as the day and the colour of summer. Now her hair was short and had changed colour with the season. She looked even better, if that were possible.

'Samantha, I almost didn't recognise you. You look well.' I didn't always mean these compliments, but where Samantha was concerned they were genuine. She ignored the praise.

'Dermot, where on earth were you? I've been looking for you everywhere.' Samantha, normally as calm as the Mediterranean, was indeed hassled, as Tommy had warned me.

'Oh, Mass and the Inns. The usual beginning-of-term routine. You know what it's like.'

'No, Dermot, I don't. I have to work for a living and I don't know anything about beginning-of-term routines.'

This wasn't the Samantha that I had come to know and love, the fun-loving, gum-chewing Samantha with not a care in the world. I knew what was wrong. Samantha was suffering from a severe dose of vacation deficit. I quickly summoned up a few holiday destinations that might be of interest to her but just as quickly thought better of it.

'Well, Samantha, what's the matter? You seem agitated.'

'I'm not agitated,' she protested, the standard reply of a person against whom such an allegation is correctly made. 'I'm just looking for my counsel.'

'Well now that you've found him, what can he do for you?'

Samantha did not waste any time. 'We're on, Dermot.'

'We're on?'

'Yes, we're on.'

'What's on?'

'Moriarty and Trinity College. Remember?'

7

Of course I did not remember. I had no idea what Samantha was talking about. Solicitors, particularly solicitors like J. Arnold O'Reilly, whose assistant Samantha is, have this belief that, once they brief counsel, the latter has every detail of the case at his fingertips on a 24/7 basis. Counsel disabuses his solicitor of this notion at his peril.

'Of course I remember it. I may be a bit rusty on the details, but the broad outline I remember well,' I said, hoping she would not ask me for even an outline of the broad outline.

'Well thank God for that anyhow,' she said.

'But before we discuss the facts of the case any further, what about the case itself?'

'As I said, Dermot, it's on.' The little mantra was back again.

'On, Samantha?'

'Yes, Dermot, on. Why do you keep repeating what I'm saying?'

'Where is it on, when is it on?' I asked, ignoring her impatience.

'Now.'

'Now?'

'There you go again, repeating what I'm saying. It's on now. N. O. W. What part of the word "now" do you not understand?'

It seemed to me that Samantha was being unnecessarily obtuse. We were in something of a cul-de-sac that we would be better out of, particularly if, as Samantha indicated, we were on *now*. Eventually I managed to extract from her that the case was in a twelve o'clock list in Court 17 before Judge Pilkington. Arnold, Samantha's boss and my best solicitor, had prevailed on the unwilling judge to put it to the end of the list but, as it was the first day of term, the list was short and it would not be long until the case would be called for the second and final time. At last the urgency was clear to me.

'But what about papers, Samantha?'

'I sent them to you, Dermot.'

'When?'

'Last week.'

'When last week?'

'Friday.'

'Friday?' What was the point of sending papers on Friday for a case on Monday?

'There you go again. Yes, Friday.'

'But how was I to get them if you only sent them on Friday?'

'Are you saying you don't have the papers?' asked Samantha, avoiding the implication of my question.

'Yes, Samantha. That's what I have been trying to tell you. I didn't know anything about the case until this moment.'

'Well, maybe if you'd been in the Library earlier instead of off gallivanting at "beginning-of-term routines", as you call them, you might have got the papers,' she retorted.

I thought it might be better if I just robed and got up to Court 17 as soon as possible. 'Perhaps if you were to give me your file I could have a look at that?' I suggested.

Samantha must have thought well of this suggestion because, no sooner had I made it than, in an apparent introduction to a warm-up routine, she brought her knee up to the level of her waist and, perching perilously in that position in the middle of the Square Hall, she rested her briefcase on her thigh and rummaged within for the elusive file. At that moment, her less-than-comprehensive skirt could have done with the extra centimetres that had been dispensed with for the summer. Samantha, of course, was oblivious.

I was quite out of breath when I reached my team outside Court 17. Arnold is never good at seeing, let alone recognising, people until they are under his nose. Happily, on account of his height, there is no difficulty in negotiating such a position.

When Samantha tipped him off that I had arrived, he thanked me for coming. 'Long vacation not long enough, Mac?' He was delighted with this combination of barb and humour. I refrained from suggesting that he should have sent the pigeon out earlier with the brief.

Arnold introduced me to our client, Professor Moriarty, who asked me if he should start at the beginning. Having regard to the limited information I had in relation to the good professor's case, there was nowhere I would have wished him to start more than at the beginning. Unfortunately, time was not on our side.

'I think it might be better if you gave me the essential details to begin with and we can fill in any gaps later,' I suggested. At that moment I had no idea what the case was about. It might have been a boundary dispute for all I knew. Hopefully not.

'As you know, Dermot ... do you mind if I call you Dermot? Thank you ... I am a professor in Trinity and on the ...' began the professor.

We were going nicely and I felt sure that, in another sixty seconds or so, I would be on top of the case. Unfortunately, it was not to be. Judge Pilkington's overbearing crier put his overbearing head around the corner and informed us in no uncertain terms that our presence was required within. I lost no time gathering Samantha's file and my team and leading both into the great judicial light.

'I see Mr McNamara coming in. Mr McNamara, are you in Moriarty *v.* Trinity College?' The judge inquired before I had time to reach the front bench.

'I am, My Lord,' I replied.

'Well it's nice of you to join us, Mr McNamara. Long vacation not long enough?' I thought it better to keep my own counsel. Arnold smiled.

'Indeed, My Lord. I do apologise. I'm afraid there was something of a breakdown in communication,' I offered.

'These things happen, Mr McNamara. Particularly after the long vacation. The important thing is that you are here now. Is your case going on?'

'It is indeed, My Lord.'

'And how long will it take?'

'Not more than an hour, My Lord. Liability is in issue, but it is quite straightforward.' Of course, it is always a mistake to commit yourself to a time, particularly on the assumption of straightforwardness.

'Well then, let's get on with it, shall we?' His Lordship urged enthusiastically, as if the sun had just come out. Things were moving a little too quickly for me. 'Getting on with it' in legal parlance meant telling the judge what the case was about. Obviously, this could not be done without at least a smattering of the facts of the case. Accordingly, I could not 'get on with it' as Judge Pilkington wished. I was beginning to feel uncomfortable.

'Well, Mr McNamara?' His Lordship had all the freshness and vitality of a sailor left off at port after a spell at sea. I suppose it was the lay-off but I was having difficulty knowing what to do. After what seemed like an eternity, I asked the Impatient One if we could have a few moments.

'What on earth for, Mr McNamara? Haven't you already had two months?' Judge Pilkington was in a sharp mood this morning.

Then it came to me in a flash. Suddenly the oil was reaching the brain cells. 'It might shorten matters, My Lord.'

If there was anything that was more likely to recommend itself to His Impatient Lordship than getting on with the case, it was the prospect of settling it. The possibility of 'shortening matters', code for settlement, was music to most judges' ears. Strictly, I suppose, I was misleading the court insofar as there was no basis for inferring that settlement might be a possibility. My forensic conscience made me look over at my opponent, Sebastian Carroll, who was representing the oldest university in the State.

Could we settle? After all, one of our recreations at coffee break was to try and remember when we last settled with Sebastian. There was nothing about Sebastian this October morning to give me encouragement. With the concentration of an artist, he was putting the finishing touches to his cross-examination. No craven settlement was going to come between Sebastian and his reputation.

'Oh yes, Mr McNamara. Quite. I see. Shorten matters. Yes. I would not like to come between two parties who wish to resolve their unhappy differences amicably.' Judge Pilkington seized the opening. Now it was the judge's turn to mislead the court. In truth, he did not care whether or not he came between the parties or whether or not they resolved their differences amicably. But if the case could be settled, that he did care about. 'Very well, Mr McNamara, do your best.'

'Your Lordship is very kind.' I waited for him to rise, which is the usual protocol in these circumstances. After a few moments, he said, 'I find that these discussions waste less time if I remain on the bench, Mr McNamara.'

'Of course, My Lord. As Your Lordship pleases.' Obviously the judge was in an even greater hurry to get home than I had thought. He did have a point. Rising for ten minutes usually turns into twenty. But His Lordship presiding over the negotiations like some earwigging owl did not help my task. I did not think that talking to my opposite number was going to help either. But I had no choice. 'Settlement, Sebastian? Any chance?' I opted for his own style – succinct.

'None,' he replied, outdoing me for succinctness.

'But this is one of your own professors,' I pleaded.

'Precisely the point, Dermot. His case is hopeless. I've told the university so. However, because of who he is they've offered half the value, but it has been refused.'

'How much?' I enquired.

'Ten thousand. It might still be there. I can enquire if you think there is any point.' I turned to Arnold and Samantha in front of me. How much more attractive Samantha was without the chewing-gum, I thought involuntarily. Even in moments of relative crisis, one can be distracted.

'Ten, Arnold. They've offered ten.'

'So they have, Mac,' Arnold replied.

'Are we not taking it?'

'No.'

'Why not?' All the time I could feel the bewigged owl's interest in our conversation.

'Your Opinion, Mac.'

'What about it?'

'Well nothing except that you said we'd win.'

'And what did I say it was worth?'

'Twenty.'

'And they've offered ten?'

'Correct.'

'Half the value?'

'Correct again, Mac. We are sharp this morning.' This was no time for what Arnold considered humour any more than it was time for me to be thinking of Samantha and her chewing-gum. Pilkington was glued to our conversation as to a ball at Wimbledon. Meanwhile, Sebastian sat impatiently.

'Could I see my Opinion please?' Of course, I didn't doubt Arnold. If that was what he said I wrote, then it was what I wrote. It's just that sometimes it is a question of emphasis or perhaps a word. Arnold passed me my letter.

Dear Arnold,

Thank you for your instructions herein. I enclose draft Civil Bill as requested.

The plaintiff's case is a strong one. Probably worth around £20,000. Unless we can get something in that ballpark, I think the case should be fought.

Yours sincerely,

Dermot

Arnold was right. Nothing could have been clearer. It was unequivocally what I said. It offended the first rule of advising: never advise unequivocally, always leave wiggle room, because things are rarely that clear. A lateral approach was required. Around the house, as it were.

'Ten is a lot of money, Arnold,' I said with the gravitas of an economist on *Questions and Answers.*

'I know, Mac, but unfortunately the professor agrees with your Opinion. Wholeheartedly.' If my letter offended the first rule, Arnold's communication of its contents to the professor offended the second (really an extension of the first): never communicate counsel's opinion to the client and, if he asks, hedge, hedge your bets. At all costs. What could I do? Which was exactly what Judge Pilkington wanted to know.

'Making progress, Mr McNamara?'

'Thank you, My Lord.'

14

'Do you think that matters will be shortened?' asked the judge, adopting my code.

'I certainly hope so, My Lord. But I will need another minute or two.'

'Just another minute or two then, Mr McNamara,' and he stuck his judicial bottom to the bench even more firmly than before, lest anyone should think that he might rise and give everyone a little space.

'Do you think there is any point in my talking to our client, Arnold?' I asked despairingly.

'None at all. His mind is quite made up.'

I turned with an even greater sense of despair to my opponent. 'Any chance of adding five, Sebastian?' I enquired, taking the risk that Sebastian might add five but that this might not satisfy the professor from Trinity.

'None,' he replied, declining my invitation with even greater clarity than my solicitor. Negotiations were at an end.

'Perhaps you would like to tell me what the case is about, Mr McNamara,' recommended Pilkington, lip-reading the situation accurately. 'I wish I could,' I almost said.

'I appear for the plaintiff,' I announced hesitantly.

'Thank you, Mr McNamara. However, we have known that for some time.'

'Of course. My Lord ... I wonder would you be kind enough to give me just a little more time?' All I knew about the case was what I had read in my letter to Arnold. By now I also had the vague recollection of a bicycle being involved.

'More time, Mr McNamara?' Judge Pilkington asked, bewildered.

'Yes, My Lord.'

'What on earth for?'

'I need to consult with my client.'

'But, Mr McNamara, you have been conducting negotiations on behalf of your client. You don't mean to tell me that you have been negotiating on behalf of your client without having consulted with him?'

'Oh no, My Lord,' I said.

'I should hope not, Mr McNamara. It would be quite improper. And as for more time, I am afraid your time has run out. It would not be fair to the other cases in the list.' Judging by the empty courtroom, it looked as if the remainder of the list had been disposed of. But I did not think this to be a wise observation. 'I must insist on your opening the case. Enough time has been wasted already.'

'Yes, My Lord,' I replied, not quite sure where to take things from here.

As I pondered my future at the Bar, Samantha passed me the Civil Bill, thereby saving my forensic bacon. Why I hadn't thought of this before, I had no idea. This document was not exactly overflowing with information about the case, but what information it had between its pages I passed on to the interested judge with suitable dollops of emphasis and intonation.

It was a learning curve for both of us. We heard of the professor's adventure in the college grounds on the previous Halloween. He was riding his bicycle on a pathway between the cricket and rugby pitches when he collided with a barrel that had a tree in it. Our professor became unstuck and the result was a serious fracture of the femur, from which he had not yet fully recovered.

I could not argue with the judicial heavyweight when he observed, 'A bit light on information, Mr McNamara?'

'I am sorry, My Lord, but I thought you might prefer to hear the evidence from the horse's mouth ... as it were.'

'No disrespect to your client of course, Mr McNamara.'

'No disrespect at all, My Lord.' I paused. 'Come up, Professor Moriarty.'

16

The professor was everything a child might imagine a professor to be. If you could conjure up a slightly more dishevelled version of Ken Dodd, you would have him in one. From the strands of hair that wandered in every direction to the leather patches on his tweed elbows, he was every inch the professor. The court registrar invited him to tell the truth, the whole truth and nothing but the truth. As he settled into the witness box, I invited him to tell His Lordship his story 'in his own words'. In this way, hopefully Judge Pilkington and I would become more familiar with the facts of his case.

'Would you like me to begin at the beginning?' the professor asked for the second time that morning, turning his academic head towards the owl.

Pilkington was astonished. It was as if the idea of beginning at the beginning was a new concept in law. 'Certainly not, Professor. That sort of thing might be fine for academia, but down here we have a day's work to do. Cases to hear, lists to clear, real lives to sort out. What chance would we have if we started everything at the beginning?'

It was the professor's turn to be astonished. The line between town and gown had never been so clearly drawn for him before. For fifty odd years he had been reasonably satisfied that he was making a contribution of sorts to society – a view clearly not shared by the luminary on the bench. 'In that event, where would you like me to begin, My Lord?' he asked.

'From what your counsel tells me, you fell off your bike. Perhaps that would be a good place to start.'

So the professor mounted his bicycle and off he cycled down the path between the two pitches, telling the judge what happened to him as he went along. Clearly, he was fussed, trying as hard as he could not to waste time or words in deference to he-who-would-adjudicate his case.

17

You could not say that the latter was inattentive. He was listening, and even taking the odd note. Somehow, however, I was not convinced that the professor had the attention he needed, or perhaps he had the attention, but not the empathy.

Samantha passed me some photographs, which, without having the opportunity to look at them myself, I handed up to the witness and through him to the judge. The professor continued his evidence, moving on to a presentation of his injuries. All the time the judge was going through the photographs.

In the middle of the professor's evidence about how he had been unable to get on a bike since the accident, the judge said, 'I am sorry to interrupt you, Professor, but would you mind turning to photograph number 11?'

The professor, who was in possession of the photographs once more, leafed through them. 'I have it, My Lord,' he cried, like a child seeking teacher's approval. Meanwhile, we were all leafing likewise. I had the uneasy feeling that we were approaching a moment of truth.

'Professor, photograph number 11 shows the barrel with which you collided. Isn't that correct?' said the judge.

'It is, My Lord.'

'In daylight. Isn't that correct?'

'It is, My Lord.'

'And photograph number 12 shows the same barrel at night. Isn't that so?'

'Indeed it is, My Lord.'

'And I assume that your case is that the lighting leaves something to be desired. Is that so?'

'It is, My Lord.'

'Well now, Professor, would you mind going back to photograph number 11? Do you see down at the bottom of the photograph, a short distance back from the barrel, there seems to be a sign. Can you see that, Professor?'

'Just about, My Lord.'

The few that were in the courtroom were completely silent. My uneasy feeling was growing.

'Can you make out what the sign says, Professor?'

Moriarty held the photograph so far away from him that he was squinting at it. Then he held it so close to him that it nearly removed one of his eyes. He was certainly doing his best. 'I am afraid I can't, My Lord.'

'I am not sure that I can myself, Professor.' I wasn't satisfied that we were getting the full story from Pilkington.

'There seems to be two words and I think that the first word may be "Cycling". But I can't make out the second,' continued the judge.

Nobody had asked Sebastian if he could make out the second word, but that did not deter him. '"Prohibited", My Lord. The sign says, "Cycling Prohibited".'

'Why thank you, Mr Carroll. God bless your eyesight. I'm sure you're right. Do you see that, Professor?'

'I am afraid I don't, My Lord. The writing is just a blur.'

'Well, Professor, let us assume for a moment that that is what the sign says. What do you think it means?'

'I beg your pardon, My Lord?'

'What do you think the sign means, Professor?'

'I assume, My Lord, it means what it says, "Cycling Prohibited".'

'That would indeed seem to follow, Professor. But, if that is correct, where does it leave your case?'

'My Lord?'

'Well, if cycling is prohibited and your case involves an accident when you were cycling where cycling is prohibited, do you think you can succeed?'

'I really have no idea, My Lord. I imagine that that is a matter for Your Lordship. But I can tell you that, when I raised the point with my solicitor, he showed me Mr McNamara's Opinion, which said that I had a strong case.'

Pilkington did not share the amusement that rippled around the courtroom. 'Professor, you are an intelligent man.'

'Thank you, My Lord.'

'And this case is not about a child in a playground. Isn't that so?'

'Quite so, My Lord.'

'Well, let me put it this way to you, Professor. You are claiming damages from your university for injuries that befell you when you had an accident while riding your bicycle in the college grounds, in an area where cycling is prohibited. Isn't that so?'

'It is, My Lord.'

'And how on earth, on the basis of those facts, do you think that you can succeed?'

'Well, when you put it like that, My Lord ...'

'For example, do you say that the sign does not apply to you?'

'No, My Lord. I mean yes, My Lord. The sign does not apply to anyone.'

'How so, Professor? Surely, if the college authorities see fit to prohibit cycling in the grounds and to erect a sign to that effect, they intend it to be obeyed?'

'All I can tell you, My Lord, is that it is not obeyed. By anyone. Students, staff, members of the public. It is as if the sign isn't there.'

'But it is there, Professor.'

'I must take Your Lordship's word for it.'

'And the photographer's word also, Professor?' There was nothing else that Moriarty could say. Pilkington had made up his mind.

'Do you wish to cross-examine?' the judge asked Sebastian, who did not have to call on much of his experience to know that cross-examination in these circumstances, however well prepared, could only be suicidal.

'No thank you, My Lord,' Sebastian replied, putting aside his notes. Seldom had success been constructed on so few words. Pilkington turned to me.

'Mr McNamara, I do not wish to cut you short.' An afternoon in the garden was looking like a real prospect for the judge.

'Of course not, My Lord.'

'I see you have witnesses in court and you are entitled to call them.'

'Thank you, My Lord.'

'But there is no point in prolonging the case unnecessarily.'

'Or flogging a dead horse,' I added, not quite as *sotto voce* as I had intended.

'I beg your pardon, Mr McNamara?'

'Nothing, My Lord. I was simply agreeing with Your Lordship.'

'Can the witnesses put your case any further, Mr McNamara?'

'Well, My Lord, I have an engineer.'

'Presumably he will say what he is expected to say?'

'Well, I don't think he would quite see it like that.'

'Of course not, but you know what I mean.'

'He will say that the barrel is a danger to cyclists at night in the absence of adequate lighting.'

'Well, let's assume for the purpose of this discussion that I accept all of that. What next? For example, what about the sign? What about the fact that cycling was prohibited?'

The fact that I had not had a consultation was a continuing disadvantage. I stared blankly at His Lordship, wondering what possible answer there could be to this incisive questioning. All the time, the settlement offer of ten thousand that was there at the start began to look like better and better value. This time it was Arnold's turn to come to the rescue. He duly leaned forward and, when my right ear was within whispering distance of him, he whispered into it.

'My Lord, Mr O'Reilly reminds me that I have a number of witnesses, students and staff, who will say that no attention was paid to this prohibition,' I said.

'That may be, Mr McNamara, and I could well see that if we were dealing with a child or even a student the practice might override the prohibition, but we're not. We are dealing with a professor of the college, someone who, for all I know, may have been a member of the committee that decided to outlaw cycling.'

'But there is no evidence of that, My Lord. None at all.'

'I know that, Mr McNamara, but you know what I mean.' Pilkington made a habit of assuming that I knew what he meant. 'It seems to me, Mr McNamara – of course I may be quite wrong, and, if I am, happily there exists a higher forum that can correct me – that Professor Moriarty cannot successfully sue his own university for an injury he sustained while riding a bicycle when he knew that cycling was prohibited.'

'But, My Lord ... forgive me for interrupting ... but there is no evidence that the plaintiff knew that cycling was prohibited.'

'Well now really, Mr McNamara, you are putting up a robust argument, but the foundations are too weak. We are, after all, living in the real world. At least some of us are,' Pilkington said, glancing over at Moriarty who was looking more and more like an extraterrestrial. 'You don't expect me to believe that a professor in his own university would not know that cycling was prohibited, now do you?' I assumed that this question from the Bench was rhetorical. 'Is there anything else you wish to add, Mr McNamara?'

'No, My Lord. Your Lordship knows my case. I can't put it any further,' I said ruefully. This judge was not for turning.

'It's not your fault, Mr McNamara. The case is unstateable. You did as much as you could. Really, it's time people took responsibility for their actions. Very well then. Dismiss the plaintiff's case. Mr Carroll, I assume you are looking for your costs?'

'Yes, My Lord.'

'That would seem to follow. What do you say, Mr McNamara?'

I was about to get to my feet to object when I noticed Sebastian's solicitor, who had represented Trinity for going on fifty years, slip him a note.

'My Lord, I have just received instructions not to seek costs, having regard to the relationship between the parties.' Sebastian sat down, clearly peeved that he had been deprived of this fruit of victory.

'That is very generous of your client, Mr Carroll. No more than I would expect. Very well then, no order as to costs.'

Pilkington consulted with the registrar about the state of the list which, despite his earlier concerns, had evaporated. He rose, bowed to those in court, and headed for his chambers and his sandwich.

'All rise. The court stands adjourned until ten thirty tomorrow morning,' the irritating crier announced, with all the solemnity of a chief justice. As we moved from the court, I could just make out the one o'clock news coming from His Lordship's transistor.

We reassembled in the corridor. The professor was not happy. 'But you told me we'd win, Arnold,' he whinged.

23

'And we will, Professor. Won't we, Mac? You said we would and we will. We will put in an appeal immediately and we will bring in Senior.'

'Who is Senior?' the professor wanted to know.

'Senior Counsel, Professor. Senior Counsel will conduct the appeal in the High Court.'

'And what happens if we draw the same judge?'

'We can't. Circuit Court, Circuit Court judge. High Court, High Court judge. Don't you give it another thought. The appeal will come up quickly and this miscarriage of justice will be undone. Isn't that right, Mac?'

One of Arnold's strengths is the fact that, because he so seldom sees the full implications of anything, he has great confidence in his opinion, which he expresses without the burden of equivocation. This is fine as long as he doesn't draw me into it, as he was now doing. The corollary of Arnold's great strength is my great weakness: seeing the implications of everything makes it difficult for me to arrive at an opinion that would be of any assistance to the client. How could one not be of the view that the fact that cycling was prohibited would have to cast a considerable cloud over the chances of a successful appeal? No one was going to thank me now or later – when we lost the appeal – for saying this. With a monumental lack of courage, I opted for later.

'Absolutely, Arnold. Absolutely,' I said, desperately trying to match Arnold's pitch of conviction.

'Well, that's decided then,' announced Arnold. 'Put in an appeal immediately, bring in Senior and hasten to the High Court.'

In that moment, the hiding we had just received at the hands of Pilkington seemed to be transformed into a victory. Samantha, the professor and Arnold went in one direction and I went in search of Mark.

*

It had been a bumpy take-off to the new term. What I had needed was a day or two to separate me from the sights and sounds of September. Rombutts with Mark would have been more suitable. It wasn't even a paying case – *pro bono*, as Rachel was never slow to remind me – unless of course our Senior brought it home in some months' time. I had my doubts.

Most barristers do the bulk of their paperwork at home. Rachel and I are no exception. For this reason, it is difficult to leave the day job fully behind you. The torture chamber, as a friend of ours insists on calling the study, is never more than a room away. Physical absence from the chamber has to be accompanied by mental absence. It isn't enough simply not to be in there.

Sharing a study works because of our different routines. Rachel is highly efficient and organised. She rises early, spends some time in the study before going into the Library and structures her day so that she has to do as little work as possible in the evening, before retiring at around nine o'clock. On the other hand, I am neither highly efficient nor organised. Even if I go to bed at nine o'clock, I cannot get up early. Usually I do my paperwork at night and this means that I get up even later. It is a vicious circle from which I am unable to escape.

One of the consequences of our respective routines is that we see little enough of one another. In an attempt to correct this, we have developed a very good habit of having a gin and tonic together before what Rachel euphemistically calls 'dinner'. This is our quality time with each other and with Kate and Conor, and of course the au pair, without whom we would definitely be doing time for child neglect. Rachel adores her children, but of course even a working mother can get too much of them.

'How did your day go, darling?' I asked Rachel, handing her a gin and tonic.

25

Swishingly, apparently. So much so that Rachel did not really need this drink. She had enjoyed the Inns – it was the best beginning of term ever – and Fleming had invited her to lunch.

Mr Justice Fleming is highly regarded as a judge of the High Court and widely regarded as having an appetite for extramarital engagements. Fleming's wife would not be everyone's choice for Ms World or indeed Mrs World, but, if that explains the enthusiasm with which he pursues the lady members of the Bar, it does not excuse it. At least it does not excuse it in the eyes of their husbands. There are few of my female colleagues whose bottoms do not bear the imprint of his hand.

Fleming was getting out of the blocks early this year. Traditionally, this lunch invitation would come later in the term, usually after a dinner in King's Inns when more is said and done by some than is prudent. I knew Rachel was well able to handle herself. Perhaps I was being complacent but, from the point of view of her affections, I doubted if, in this instance at least, her interest went beyond the political.

'And yours, darling. How was your day?' Rachel asked. Already I was regretting having initiated this topic of conversation. I had hardly told Rachel about heading for a Rombutts with Mark and being called urgently by Samantha, when she said, 'Not another *pro bono*, Dermot?'

'Afraid so. For the moment anyway. Worst start to the term ever. Pilkington would not give me time for a consultation. He made me go on, so I had to make it up as I went along. Some professor in Trinity fell off his bike. Seemed an OK case. But there was a "Cycling Prohibited" sign and that was that. Pilkington wouldn't hear another word. Wanted to know if the professor could read.'

'Doesn't seem unreasonable to me. Anyway, you know my views on these personal injury cases. They shouldn't

26

be in the courts at all. Waste of valuable court time and taxpayers' money.'

I didn't want a row. 'Anyway, Rach, Arnold is intent on appealing it. Says he'll bring in Senior.'

'Really, Dermot, you'll have to expand a bit. Arnold is a messer. Does your reputation no good. You'll have to find some new solicitors.'

Rachel was right, but I was in no humour to concede. 'That's not fair on Arnold. He has been very good to me. Anyway, how do you find new solicitors?'

'Socialise a bit more. Downstairs. Blackhall Place. The Shelbourne. You know the scene.'

'Touting, Rachel, that's what you mean, isn't it?'

'No, I don't mean touting. I mean networking, advertising your product. Even the Bible encourages it: "Don't hide your light under a bushel."' She took a sip of her gin and tonic and changed the subject. 'Who do you think he'll bring in as Senior?'

'Senior? Oh yes, the appeal. Margaret, of course. He's very keen on Margaret. Professionally, I mean.'

'Of course, professionally,' Rachel said with heavy sarcasm.

'You don't think there could be anything between Arnold and Margaret, do you?'

'No, I don't,' Rachel replied. 'In fact, I don't think there could be anything between Arnold and anyone.' She paused. 'What about me, Dermot?'

'You? You and Arnold?'

'No, silly. Arnold briefing me?'

'Instead of me?' I asked, feeling that I was missing the point.

'Heavens, Dermot, we are slow tonight. No wonder you lost the professor's case. As a Senior.'

'But you're not a Senior,' I replied pedantically.

'Ah, we're warming up. It's a wonder the case finished today.' She paused. 'Fleming says I should take silk.'

'Fleming? What would he know about it?' I was taken aback.

'He was quite serious. Said that was why he invited me to lunch. Wanted to ring me over the vacation. He thinks there is an opening for a new Senior. Believes that the quality of the Senior Bar is at an all-time low and needs new talent. Especially female talent. Someone like me.'

'Now, Rachel, you know why Fleming wants to invite you to lunch and it has nothing to do with taking silk.'

'Now, now, Dermot, no need to be jealous.'

'Jealous, Rachel? Jealous? Who? Me? Of whom? Fleming?'

'He's not the worst. Bit bald perhaps. But at least he's not as stuffy as most of them.'

'They're all the same,' I said huffily, feeling that the evening was no improvement on the day. Rachel McNamara, S.C.? Hmmm ... I wasn't sure that I was ready for this development.

Kate and Conor were playing away happily. The au pair was enjoying her gin and tonic. To be fair, usually they got more of a look in. First day back and all that.

ECUMENICAL AFFAIRS

He is perhaps the outstanding advocate of his generation. Tall and well built, he could have played for the All Blacks were it not for the fact that he was from the wrong hemisphere and ... he preferred music. To rugby. Indeed, to everything. He prefers music to everything.

He is idiosyncratic. He wears his head at a tilt and tweed jackets at weekends. He walks everywhere. Frequently, of a Saturday or Sunday, you can see him bestriding the city bearing large brown envelopes full of treasured Opinions or heftily marked briefs. These he deposits in the polished letterboxes of offices whose owners are at home with their wives and families. He doesn't have a wife. Instead, he chooses to spend his time playing the violin in his apartment overlooking Merrion Square.

All day, every day, he is in court. His substantial practice is, like eggs, free-range, recognising neither physical nor intellectual boundary. He travels up and down the spectrum of law and country; though to keep him out of his apartment in Merrion Square will cost you. Seldom will you find him in the Law Library after ten past four, the extra ten minutes allowing him just enough time to remove his wig and gown and gather his briefs for the following day. Except, for what reason I have never found out, on the last day of term. On that day, when the rest of his profession are dotted around the culinary hotspots of the capital celebrating the arrival of the most recent

29

vacation, he is stuck to his seat in the Library until after six. On that afternoon he would get through hundreds of pages of briefs, making an occasional note, interrupted from time to time by the good wishes of the privileged few who know him well enough to disturb this industry. He is known for a prodigious memory and the speed at which he devours papers.

He is a man of few words. 'That's a' are two of his favourites. He likes to use them often and consecutively. The record, which stands at twenty, was nearly broken one day when, to my surprise, he stood up to acknowledge and congratulate me in the one gesture.

When Mark came over to congratulate me on the arrival of our twins, I had been sitting opposite Richard Thornton, S.C. for some time. A few friends had assembled around me, and Richard, sensing a celebration, was overtaken by a desire to play his part. He rose to his feet and, knowing neither me nor the reason for the celebration, outstretched his hand. I was flattered and wondered what nice words of congratulation he might offer me.

'That's a,' he commenced. 'That's a,' he continued. 'That's a ... that's a ... that's a ...' he carried on, until at last he resumed his seat, uttering one final definitive 'that's a' before immersing himself once again in his all-consuming brief.

*

It was Friday morning of the third week of term. I was running a little late. Rachel had left for work at dawn. With poor timing, our daughter Kate waited until after her mother had left to be sick; though, in fairness, whether she became ill before or after her mother left would not have impacted significantly on her mother's schedule. Happily, our family doctor is only around the corner and health or at least the promise of it was restored to the household without too much delay.

When I got into the Library, I looked in my pigeonhole en route to my desk as usual. Time was, not so long ago, I would approach the pigeonhole with anticipation tinged with ever-increasing pessimism, as day after empty day it lay bare. Even now, when things were considerably better, the empty pigeonhole still made me nervous. And if it was empty two days in a row, this was a cause for serious introspection.

An Post recognises many different categories of mail but, for the barrister, there are only three. There is the small envelope through which you can feel the staple securing the cheque. This envelope is always welcome. In truth, I may greet it more with relief than celebration as, more than likely, the money has already been spent many times over.

Secondly, there is the new set of instructions. Again, always welcome. No matter how busy the barrister becomes, no matter how inundated with paperwork, he never ceases to thank God for the fact that there are solicitors out there who wish to brief him. 'May the pigeonhole spilleth over rather than be bare' is the motto.

And of course there is *the reminder*. The dreaded reminder, distinguishable from the cheque only by the absence of a staple: 'Dear Mr McNamara, it is now three months since my original instructions. Please return the papers.' And so the alarm goes off at five in the morning and the ravings of a restless sleep are distilled into a heartless dictaphone, as you desperately try to pacify an irate solicitor.

On this Friday morning the entire of my pigeonhole was taken up with a blockbuster of a brief. It was immediately obvious that it did not come from the office of J. Arnold O'Reilly, Solicitor, on the third floor of 203 Gardiner

Street. Arnold's office would have neither the resources nor the inclination to put such a magnificent brief together. Arnold is definitely from the *nouvelle cuisine* school of briefing: less is more. So, if the brief wasn't from Arnold, then who was it from?

I carried the brief to my desk with reverence. Slowly, painstakingly, I unsealed the envelope, curiosity vying with excitement. Rachel was going to like this one. It was from Walsh & Phillips of Fitzwilliam Square, no less. This was something of a red-letter day. A brief from a new solicitor is always a source of particular pleasure. Strictly, this was not a new solicitor. I immediately recalled a case I had done for this office two years earlier: Walsh, Hogan, Murray-Maguire & Phillips as they were then. I had no idea what had happened to the middle two in the meantime.

On that occasion, I had my colleague Frank to thank for a last-minute handover. Frank is not known for handovers and certainly not good ones, so it was a surprise. I remembered the case well. It concerned the wonderful showjumper, Penelope Jones. What a win, and against the odds. Frank was furious and, needless to say, the handovers dried up. Not even a building contract. I have to say I was surprised that Mr Phillips, my briefing solicitor, had not been back for my services either. He was so pleased at the time. I didn't receive another brief and, come to think of it, I didn't get a cheque either. Money in the bank it might have been, but it wasn't in my bank. Anyway, I decided not to allow the joy of the moment be tarnished by unseemly petulance.

I fingered the elegant brief with the same pride and affection that a sculptor might bestow on his creation. It consisted of two red folders, each packed with pages separated by dividers, each divider sporting a coloured flag with its very own letter of the alphabet. It was a pleasure to turn the pages. This was good news, good news indeed, and I wanted to share it at the first opportunity with Mark and, of course, Frank.

'Congratulations, Mac,' Mark offered magnanimously when I told him. 'You have finally arrived.' A brief from Fitzwilliam Square is every barrister's dream and I had received it, albeit at last, in my own right. The coffee rarely tasted so good.

The barristers' restaurant was packed and buzzing. Early morning consultations had been concluded, judges had been told what cases were going on and how long they would take, and now the forensic surgeons were exchanging end-of-week gossip before continuing their day's work.

'Who's your Senior?' Afric wanted to know after Mark had explained why congratulations were in order.

'Richard Thornton,' I replied.

'Wow,' exclaimed Afric. 'A brief from Walsh & Phillips and led by Thornton. Now that *is* something.' With which bouquet Afric leaned over and gave me a kiss on my blushing cheek.

'Haven't had a chance to see what it's about yet other than it's a libel action for next Tuesday,' I informed them. 'A lot of reading. So much for my weekend, I suppose.'

But, of course, I didn't mind.

*

Arnold phoned the following Monday evening. 'Is that you, Mac?'

There was a reasonable chance that it was me alright. Unless Rachel was having an affair and bringing him home.

'Brief for tomorrow, Mac. See you in the morning?' As ever, last-minute notification, dearth of detail and assumption of my availability. I barely managed to respond before he put the phone down.

'Eh, Arnold, I'm afraid I can't.'

'What do you mean you can't?'

'Just that. I can't. I have a libel action in the High Court.' I was just informing Arnold as to the factual reason for my unavailability. I wasn't trying to impress him, which was just as well because I wasn't succeeding.

'So?'

'So what, Arnold?'

'Haven't you got a Senior?'

'As a matter of fact I have, but I'm expected to be there.'

Arnold was not rolling over on this one. 'Who is your Senior, Mac?' It was none of his business.

'Richard Thornton.'

'And do you think Thornton won't be able to manage without you?' Arnold asked.

'Not for a moment, but ...' I wanted to explain that I thought it was probably in the best interests of my recently acquired Fitzwilliam Square practice that I be there ... without of course offending my Gardiner Street one.

'Not good enough for you, Mac, is that it?' Arnold asked, reading my mind.

'Not at all, Arnold. And of course you're right – Richard is well able to handle it on his own. But I am briefed in it after all and I think that my solicitor and my client expect me to be there.' I hoped that that would do it.

'Not impressed, Mac. Must never forget those who started you off. Unavailability is the first step to unemployment. That's what I say.'

It looked as if I was going to need my Fitzwilliam Square practice, even if I was overestimating its interest in me.

'I'm sorry, Arnold. I usually am available. I would love to do your case, but just this once I really think I have no option but to decline.'

Usually, of course, if there is a clash due to a last minute phone call from Arnold, I would be able to take the case on anyway. More than likely it would be a Circuit Court action in the same court or, if not, in a neighbouring one and I could take a chance.

This was different. There were a number of distinguishing features but, in truth, the telling one was the fact that I did not think it would impress Mr Phillips if, on what was in effect my first outing on behalf of Fitzwilliam Square, I did not show my face until four o'clock and then only to enquire as to the fees. Of course, Arnold was not listening to a word I said.

'Very well, Mac. It's your decision,' he said, making it quite clear what he thought of it. 'Who will I get at this hour?' I heard him ask as he put down the phone.

The call was not inducing a feel-good factor on this Monday evening, but time was not on my side and I had no alternative but to put Arnold and my erstwhile Gardiner Street practice out of my mind, my children to bed and devote the remaining hours to the exclusive preparation of Sorenson *v. The Irish Daily News*.

*

Two years earlier I had walked in the rain from the Dart station to Mr Phillips's office for a consultation in the Penelope Jones case. On this occasion, Rachel left me to the hall door and, if she could have driven her convertible Golf into reception, she would have done so.

The early birds were already typing away. Even at the early hour of eight thirty the office was a hive of activity. The twenty-four hour day had not yet arrived in Dublin for offices, but I reckoned that many of the people I was encountering were well into the second half of their working day.

'Dermot McNamara,' I announced to the pretty receptionist who was not chewing gum. 'Could I see Mr Phillips please?'

'Is he expecting you?' she enquired, somewhat sceptically. It seemed unlikely that I was just dropping in to see Mr Phillips in his office in Fitzwilliam Square at this hour of the morning without an appointment. This wasn't Main Street, Ballydehob after all.

'I hope so,' I replied.

'What did you say your name was again?'

I repeated my name, at the same time resolving that the day would come when she would not have to ask even once.

'If you would like to take a seat, Mr Phillips's personal assistant will be with you in a moment.'

Perhaps I had got the wrong Tuesday. At least when you went to Arnold's office you could see from the reception area whether or not he was there.

I waited for about ten minutes. The reading material was even more boring, if that were possible, than at the dentist's. *Business & Finance* was open on the coffee table at the page that showed Walsh & Phillips's name at the top of the Best Solicitors List. I held my brief closer to my chest.

Eventually, Mr Phillips's personal assistant arrived and marched me through labyrinthine corridors and up several floors until we reached the Daniel O'Connell Room, where they have their most important meetings.

'Welcome on board,' Mr Phillips greeted as he shook my hand. 'Thank you for stepping into the breach.' The Junior Counsel who was in the case originally had taken silk recently – hence the breach into which I was only too happy to step. What happened to Frank? I wondered.

'Barbara, I would like you to meet Mr McNamara, our distinguished Junior Counsel.' I looked around quickly to see if anyone else had entered the room.

36

Barbara Sorenson was considerably better looking than the photograph that adorned her column suggested. Usually it was vice-versa. We shook hands. I was re-introduced to Amy and Sophie, the beautiful apprentices who had helped me with the Penelope Jones case when Phillips disappeared for a few hours to conduct a merger and acquisition of the entire South African corporate world. I was surprised that they were still here. Presumably a slight hiccup on the examination front.

Suddenly I felt a tightness in the pit of my stomach. Where on earth was Richard Yehudi Thornton, S.C.? After all, this was Walsh & Phillips, the top solicitors firm in Ireland. And this was Barbara Sorenson, the well-known ecumenical affairs correspondent with the *Catholic Times*, and we were only two hours away from the kick-off to what would undoubtedly be the libel action of the season. Surely I wasn't going to have to conduct the consultation? Of course, I had been up half the night reading the papers and could recite the facts of the case as well as I ever recited *Paradise Lost* or *Paradise Regained*, but libel actions are different. There are twists and turns and nuances ... in addition to which I had not done one before. The exclusive attention of Richard Thornton, S.C. was most definitely required.

'Barbara, Mr Thornton said he might be delayed,' Phillips explained and turned to me. 'Dermot, over to you. Where would you like to begin?'

All, including it seemed the frowning fathers who looked down on us from their dull frames, turned in my direction. Before I had a chance to suggest 'the beginning', there was a knock on the door and in walked the Great One. I was sure that my sigh of relief was audible. There were more introductions.

'Richard, of course you know your Junior?' Phillips said.

'Yes, indeed. Good morning, David. I know David well. In fact we sit opposite one another in the Library.' Half right. We did sit opposite one another but David was the name of the Junior who had created the breach into which I was happy to step. I said nothing.

We sat in silence for some, followed by many, moments. This time everyone was looking at Richard who, head at a tilt, was looking down at his brief with its traditional pink ribbon. Mark had told me about this: Richard is very comfortable with silence. His ability to remain mute for considerable lengths of time, even when people are looking to him for leadership, is legendary and I was getting my first taste of it.

For a moment I was worried because I thought that Phillips might again turn to me. But no, this time Phillips opened. He brought us up to date on recent developments and then asked Barbara if she would tell Mr Thornton her story in her own words. The occasional 'that's a' was as much as we heard from Richard and, when Barbara ran out of things to say, he suggested that we reconvene at half past ten outside Court 4. My leader declined Phillips's offer of a lift, saying he had a number of errands to run on the way down.

'Doesn't say much, does he?' Barbara observed after Richard left the room.

'No, Barbara,' Phillips replied as he watched the October sun light up the tennis court in the square below. 'No, he doesn't.' Clearly, he too was affected by Richard's economy of words.

*

I was in a state of high excitement. The Round Hall was packed as usual by half past ten on Tuesday morning. The personal injury list was being called over in Court 1, a murder case was resuming in Court 2 and the president of the High Court was calling over the jury list in Court 4.

The Four Courts was one place in the land in which one could smoke with impunity and indeed with justification. After all, in one court, a person's liberty, if not his life, was at stake. In another, the entire spectrum of personal injuries was about to be litigated, with recovering patients, plaintiffs for a day, in pursuit of pots of gold. In our court, our client would seek to convince her husband and a jury that her marital integrity was intact. Each case had its team of barristers, solicitors and witnesses and, for the duration, these would be as intimately linked to the ups and downs of the cases as the parties themselves. Were they not entitled to their fix of nicotine without fear of fine?

Richard was in the front bench reserved for Senior Counsel, informing His Presidential Lordship that his case was going on and would take the rest of the week. The president said that he would take up the case at eleven after the jury had been sworn, whereupon Richard led Phillips, Amy, Sophie and me out of the courtroom and into the Round Hall beneath the dome.

It could have been Croke Park, such was the din. Had Richard been minded to share some words of wisdom, we would have been hard put to hear them.

'What happens now, Dermot?' Barbara asked.

I never like questions being addressed to me when my Senior is present. For one thing, the answer I give might be wrong, but also it might not be consistent with the Senior's plan for the case. If that was how I felt with Seniors generally, it was magnified many times when the Senior from whose shadow I was being lured was that of Richard Thornton. However, Barbara's question didn't appear to have too many pitfalls. I looked over at Richard who was staring at the floor a few feet in front of him, occasionally raising his eyes just enough to survey the hall.

'Well, the usual thing is that negotiations take place,' I ventured. 'The defendant's counsel will want to know how much we are looking for and, when Richard tells him, he will be in a position to formulate an offer.' I didn't think that I had put either the case or my reputation at risk with this reply. Nonetheless, I thought it might not be any harm to obtain my leader's imprimatur. 'What do you think, Richard?' He didn't think anything apparently. He just stood there, that enigmatic smile on his face, leaving my question in mid-air.

At that moment, J.J. Jones, S.C. emerged from the throng of witnesses and lawyers. 'Good Morning, Richard,' Jones greeted.

'That's a,' Richard replied, and the two leaders disappeared into the throng. Paradoxically, in this most public of places they could find the privacy that their negotiations required.

If Richard enjoys the paramount reputation in the Law Library, Jones is not far behind, with a few years in hand. Whereas Richard is well built, Jones has the physique of a greyhound. He is thin, short and compact. Nothing is wasted. If he smiles, and he doesn't smile often, it is by way of warning rather than welcome. There may not be much in it but, if anything, Richard is the warmer of the two.

From our distance we watched these two giants of the Bar in what was as animated a negotiation as they were capable of. As one might expect, it didn't last long. We tried to discern the outcome of the negotiations from Richard's demeanour as he wove his way back to his fold, but without success.

'We will be going on,' he announced to his acolytes as he swept into Court 4. What seemed to be the entire attendance of the Round Hall swept in after him.

It was one minute to eleven. There wasn't a seat left in the house, with one exception of course. Below the seat reserved for the president of the High Court, the registrar Ms Devine was putting the finishing touches to whatever registrars put the finishing touches to moments before the off. Below Ms Devine and on the left wing of the court sat Phillips, flanked by Amy and Sophie. Opposite Phillips and facing the as-yet-empty seat was Richard, behind whose ample frame I was happy to shelter. On his right crouched Jones, like an athlete at the start of an Olympic final. Across from Jones, his solicitor; behind Jones, his Junior Counsel. Behind us all, a host of devils, fresh as daffodils, were sprinkled around the courtroom waiting for the master class to begin. The pews on the right wing of the court were crowded with journalists.

As the bride's guests sit behind the bride and the groom's guests behind the groom, so Barbara, the plaintiff in this action, sat with her husband behind her legal team, and Thompson of the defendant newspaper sat behind his.

Thompson, a high-profile journalist with the *Irish Daily News*, had penned the offending article a year or so before and if, with the passage of time, he had any misgivings about what he had written, they were not obvious from his confident demeanour. Sporting a bright bow-tie and a bold-striped suit, he looked more like a candidate for Leopardstown than the defendant's enclosure in the Four Courts. Perhaps Leopardstown was on the cards come four o'clock.

In a raised box overlooking these last-minute preparations sat the six men and six women who would decide Barbara's case. The perfumed conversations of those members of the public who were there out of curiosity vied with the professional conversations of clients and lawyers for the attention of the jurors.

'All rise!' announced the crier. On the dot of eleven, the door to the judge's chambers opened and, to our surprise, who emerged onto the bench only the energetic and punctual Mr Justice Fleming. Who knew what had happened to the president in the meantime? The last seat was taken and the show was ready to begin.

'Good morning, Ms Devine,' said the judge to the registrar, already giving the impression that he had been incarcerated in his chambers for too long.

'Good morning, Judge,' returned Ms Devine with a pleasant smile.

'Good morning, ladies and gentlemen,' greeted his Lordship as he surveyed the courtroom. This was a rhetorical greeting. Of course, the jury was not to know this and, to a man and a woman, the jury wished the judge many happy returns.

'Good news, David,' my leader informed me, referring to the change of judge. 'Fleming is as partial to publicity as he is to good-looking women ... can't do us any harm.' I was flattered by Richard taking me into his confidence. With a bit of luck he would get my name right sooner rather than later.

'Sorenson *v. The Irish Daily News*,' announced the divine registrar.

'Well, Mr Thornton,' Fleming said, looking down at Richard, who was on his feet.

'That's a' he said a few times and then continued. 'I appear for the plaintiff in this case, My Lord ... that's a ... with ... that's a ... Mr ... that's a ...' I wasn't sure that he was going to get through this and, if he did, that he would get my name right, 'that's a ... Mr ... that's a ... McNamara.' Such sweet music to my ears. My proudest moment in a wig and gown. I tried to look as if this was a typical Tuesday morning.

After Richard, Jones was on his feet giving the judge similar information from his side's point of view. At least I assumed he was. For just a few moments the successful career that beyond a doubt now lay ahead of me flashed before my eyes and I was oblivious to what was going on. I hardly heard the judge address me.

'Mr McNamara?'

'Yes, My Lord.' I wasn't expecting to be catapulted so suddenly into the limelight. Why on earth was he looking at me? Richard turned around, whispered a few 'that's a's' into my ear and I rose to my feet.

'Of course, My Lord,' I managed to utter as I sought to regain my composure and the appearance of one who knew what he was at.

In the legal long-ago, there was a practice, now honoured more in the breach, whereby Junior Counsel would 'open the pleadings'. It wasn't *Hamlet*, but it involved introducing the jury to the legal documents in the case wherein each party set out his stall. In recent times, this role has been diluted and all that remains of it is for Junior Counsel to rise to his inexperienced feet, announce to the utterly perplexed members of the jury in front of him that he is 'formally opening the pleadings' and sit down. Not much of a part perhaps, but there for what it is worth.

Such was my surprise at being addressed by the judge that I was deep in my dissertation to the jury on the legal documents in the case before I realised to my horror that I was exceeding my brief. Just as surely as the jury had no idea what I was talking about, they had no idea that the exercise I was engaged in was by now no more than an anachronism. The same could not be said of His Impatient Lordship, my leader in front of me and all my know-all colleagues beaming like lighthouses around the court.

There was only one thing for it – blunder on as if wiser words had rarely been spoken. Eventually, I stumbled on the last document and, taking out my handkerchief, sat down. This job normally takes thirty seconds. I had been at it for ten minutes; it must have been nearly lunchtime. I was exhausted.

Not one to miss a sitter like this, Fleming, turning to my leader, said, 'Not much left in the case, Mr Thornton. Would you like to go straight into evidence?'

'Thank you, My Lord ... that's a ... I think ... that's a ... I would like to address the jury.'

'Very well, Mr Thornton. The floor is yours.'

Richard rose and turned towards the jury. Without a note, without a pause for words, unless you counted the countless 'that's a's' sprinkled throughout his speech, he outlined Ms Sorenson's case to the jury. It was a triumph of storytelling. For twenty minutes he held the jury enthralled. 'Perhaps it is not the most serious defamation to come before these courts,' he told them, 'but, none-theless, it is a matter of no little consequence.'

In a delightfully understated way, the jury was left in no doubt that substantial damages would have to be awarded. If they had known nothing of Barbara's private persona and little enough of her public one twenty minutes earlier, after Richard's discourse to them her past, present and future must have been imprinted on their imaginations as indelibly as if she was a much loved family member.

'With your permission, My Lord ... that's a ... I will ... that's a ... call Ms Sorenson.' Richard turned his back on the judge and, with a commanding wave of his hand, summoned the journalist to her rightful place at the top of the court.

The courtroom was so packed that it was with difficulty that she made her way to the witness box. She had a good sense of theatre and was in no hurry. All eyes were on this attractive woman in her mid-forties as she passed beneath the jury box. Her appearance belied her occupation. The ecumenical affairs correspondent for the *Catholic Times* climbed the few steps to the stand where so many plaintiffs had gone before.

There was nothing reluctant about her procession through the courtroom, nor her ascent to the witness box. Indeed, quite the contrary. Her demeanour suggested relish and confidence. Her right hand did not shake as she held the Bible and there was no hint of hesitation in her voice as she swore to Almighty God. A discreet tug of her skirt as she sat down, and Mr Justice Fleming was in like a shot.

'Ms Sorenson, just sit down there and make yourself comfortable. You have nothing to be nervous about.'

Barbara looked as if she had never been nervous in her life. 'Thank you, My Lord,' she said, giving His Caring Lordship the benefit of exclusive eye contact. If she hadn't met Fleming before, she had met many like him.

Richard took Barbara through the evidence that had caused right-thinking people to think less of her. She was a perfect witness: female, forty, flirtatious. She flirted, but not excessively, first with Fleming and then the jury. She even had a go with Richard. Anyone who didn't know him better might have believed that he was delighted with her attentions, but Richard was a professional to his fingertips and there could be no doubt that he would go to sleep that night thinking of a Beethoven violin concerto rather than Barbara Sorenson. As he resumed his seat, the jury must have been wondering if, in his opening address, he had undersold her case.

Barbara forgot, or perhaps chose to give that impression, that she had yet to be cross-examined, and made to leave the witness box.

'If you wouldn't mind staying where you are for a moment or two *Miss* Sorenson,' requested Jones as he rose to his feet. 'I just have one or two questions to ask you if you don't mind.'

'Of course, Mr Jones. I would be delighted,' replied a compliant Barbara.

'Thank you, Miss Sorenson,' said Jones.

'Thank you indeed, Ms Sorenson,' said Fleming. 'As you may not know, Mr Jones is entitled to cross-examine you, but there is nothing to worry about. The days when cross-examination was something to be feared are long since gone. Thankfully we live in more civilised times. Mr Jones is a thorough gentleman. Mr Thornton is here to protect you … and of course Mr McNamara … and, in the unlikely event of their leaving anything through, I am, as it were, in goal.' A broad beam in Barbara's direction indicated that Fleming had concluded his soothing words.

'Thank you, My Lord,' Barbara said demurely.

'Your witness, Mr Jones.'

Jones was not pleased. 'Before commencing my cross-examination, My Lord, I wish to make the point that I do not think this witness needs quite as much protection as Your Lordship seems keen to bestow upon her. From what we have seen in her answers to Mr Thornton, she is well able to handle herself.'

'Carry on, Mr Jones,' urged Fleming as he beamed once more at Barbara. Jones paused and then continued.

'*Miss* Sorenson, you have told us that you are now, and have been for more than two years, the ecumenical affairs correspondent for the *Catholic Times*. Isn't that right?' Jones's questions were asked with the precision of a neurosurgeon and the detachment of a pathologist. He didn't ask his meticulously carved questions to curry favour with anyone, not the judge, his solicitor or his client. He asked them because it was his job to ask them and he did so in the manner in which he did because it was the only way he knew.

'It is, Mr Jones.'

'And that you are a practising Catholic, isn't that so?'

'It is, Mr Jones.'

'And that you are happily married, isn't that also correct?'

'As you say, Mr Jones, that is also correct.'

'And that you have been happily married for some years?'

'Right again, Mr Jones.'

'And that you were greatly distressed when you read Mr Thompson's article in which it was stated that, before you became ecumenical affairs correspondent for the *Catholic Times*, you were involved in "other types of affairs" and had "played away from home" on several occasions?'

'I couldn't believe my eyes. Yes, as you say, I was greatly distressed. As was my husband. Wouldn't you be, Mr Jones?'

'If you don't mind, *Miss* Sorenson, I'll ask the questions.'

'Of course. I'm sorry.'

'Would it be fair to say that, some time before you became ecumenical affairs correspondent for the *Catholic Times*, you experienced something of a conversion on the road to Damascus?'

'I can assure you that I was never in Damascus, Mr Jones.' A titter went around the courtroom. Fleming joined in.

'I think you know what I mean,' Jones said, adding a cube of ice.

'Do I, Mr Jones?'

'My point is that you were heading towards Damascus – metaphorically speaking – when you had a Pauline conversion and, as a result, never actually reached your destination. You u-turned as it were. Is that correct?'

'I'm not quite sure that I'm with you, Mr Jones,' Barbara responded.

'Nor I, Mr Jones,' interposed His Lordship.

'Nor I, My Lord,' Richard said, adding his weight.

'It will become clear, My Lord. Very clear. Very soon,' Jones reassured everyone.

'The sooner the better, Mr Jones. I am sure that the jury dislikes mysteries just as much as I do.'

'This at least, My Lord, is a mystery that we will all understand.'

'Please continue, Mr Jones.'

'What I am getting at, Miss Sorenson, as I think you know very well, is that, before becoming ecumenical affairs correspondent, you were a very different type of correspondent for a very different type of newspaper. Isn't that so?'

'I wrote a social column once a week for the *Irish Daily News* if that's what you mean, Mr Jones.'

'It's precisely what I mean. However, to adorn your creativity with the title "social column" is perhaps to confer on it a status it does not deserve?'

'I don't agree, Mr Jones. It was indeed a social column. Fortunately not everyone wants to spend their time reading law reports or *Business & Finance*. There are many ordinary people in the world. I wrote about what interested them – social matters, parties, openings of art exhibitions, book launches, that sort of thing. What was happening in the real world.'

'With scant regard for the truth, isn't that right, Miss Sorenson?' Jones asked in the same monotone as he pushed the cross-examination into a higher gear. He could have been asking her how often she had been to St Peter's.

Richard was on his adversarial feet immediately. 'My Lord ... that's a ... I must object ... that's a ... to ... that's a ... my friend's line of cross-examination. I was about to

... that's a ... interrupt earlier but it wasn't clear where the cross-examination was leading, but now ... that's a ... it is ... that's a ... all too clear.'

'What precisely are you objecting to, Mr Thornton?' Fleming wanted to know.

'What Ms Sorenson did before she became ecumenical affairs correspondent for the *Catholic Times* is of no matter. In a word, that's a ... it is ... that's a ... irrelevant. The fact that she is now ecumenical affairs correspondent is also irrelevant. What is relevant is that Mr Thompson has written these plainly defamatory words about her. When he wrote ... that's a ... that she "played away from home", when he wrote ... that's a ... that she was "involved in other types of affairs", he defamed her. What has her previous life as a social columnist got to do with anything? In my respectful submission ... that's a ... this line of cross-examination ought not to be allowed.'

'I am inclined to agree with Mr Thornton,' Fleming said, none too surprisingly.

There is a school of lawyers that believes in a sycophantic approach to the bench. Jones is not of that school. He rose to join the fray. 'My Lord, I am surprised at my friend's objection and, frankly, more surprised by your support of it. It is difficult in a case of this nature to imagine a line of cross-examination that is more relevant. I will be adducing evidence to justify the words written of course, but, in the unlikely event that this leg of my defence is unsuccessful, I submit that, in order to be awarded damages, the plaintiff must, as a matter of law, establish that she has a reputation in the first place. On behalf of the defendant I submit she has no such reputation and this line of cross-examination is in this context. If Your Lordship considers this argument even for a moment, you will see that this line of cross-examination is unassailable.' Jones resumed his seat.

'Well, gentlemen, I can see that this is a very important issue in the case and, since Mr Jones suggests I should give it more thought, I will do just that. Will we say two o'clock?' Fleming announced. It was only a quarter to one, but no one was going to object to an extra fifteen minutes for lunch.

'All rise. The court stands adjourned to two o'clock,' Fleming's crier chanted and His Lordship headed for the wings.

'I hope he doesn't allow Jones to pursue this line of cross-examination,' Phillips said as we headed out into the Round Hall. 'What do you think, Richard?'

'Quite the contrary, Phillips, quite the contrary. That's a ... he must allow him as a ... that's a ... matter of law and I hope he does. Fleming is no fool.'

If Phillips wasn't quite sure where this little rider to Richard's opinion left him, he chose not to pursue it. Instead, he headed over to Barbara and I headed down for lunch.

'Heard you addressed the jury, Mac,' Frank announced as we dived into our bangers and chips. There were roars of laughter as he recounted my faux pas. It wasn't often that I was in the case of the moment and I was enjoying every minute of it, even if just now it was at my expense.

'Wouldn't you think Thornton would have introduced that bit about Sorenson's former career? To take the sting out of it?' asked Cormac, who fancied himself as knowing something about the dynamics of libel actions.

'Jones wouldn't miss an opportunity like that,' Afric added.

'I'm not sure,' Mark rejoined. 'My money's on Thornton. I know Jones is good, but in my view Thornton would screw him and he wouldn't even know he had been screwed.'

I left them to their opinions and their leisurely lunch and ran off to the afternoon session.

At precisely two o'clock Fleming burst back onto the bench, his enthusiasm for life restored by a sandwich from the local Spar. He probably still missed the bangers and chips from the barristers' restaurant, but that was one of the sacrifices you had to make when you went up. He wished everyone a good afternoon and the jury returned the greeting. The registrar called the name of the case and the afternoon's proceedings began.

'I have considered the issues raised by Mr Jones's line of cross-examination over lunch,' said Fleming. 'I have considerable sympathy for Mr Thornton's objection, but I have come to the conclusion that, in this instance, Mr Jones is correct. There is no need for me to remind Mr Jones of the dangers inherent in the route he is taking.'

'None at all, My Lord. But I am grateful to Your Lordship for alluding to them,' Jones responded with a steely smile. Phillips sought reassurance from Richard who, inscrutable as ever, looked down at the still unopened brief in front of him.

'Ms Sorenson ... that's a ...' Richard invited Barbara back for afternoon tea with Jones.

'My Lord, before I resume my cross-examination of the plaintiff, there is a matter that I wish to mention to you in the absence of the jury,' announced Jones.

'Very well, Mr Jones. Ladies and gentlemen of the jury, I apologise for this inconvenience. As you have heard, Mr Jones has a matter he wishes to discuss with me. As more than likely it is a legal matter, it is appropriate that it should be discussed in your absence. Accordingly, could I ask you to retire to your room? I am sure this will not take long.' One by one the seats of the jurors snapped up and they vacated their box.

'Well, Mr Jones?' There was a tension in the air, an acute curiosity as to what Jones was up to.

'My Lord, I hesitate to make this point but I am under strict instructions to do so.'

'Mr Jones, you are either making the point or you are not. Whether or not it is accompanied by hesitation on your part is not of any import. Please let us hear it.'

'I am instructed that Mr Phillips had lunch with the plaintiff,' said Jones, grasping the nettle.

'So, Mr Jones?' responded a puzzled Fleming. Whether he was really puzzled or was just making it more difficult for Jones to make his hesitant point was not clear.

'Mr Phillips is her solicitor,' Jones added, to clarify matters.

'So, Mr Jones?' Fleming asked again, matters unclarified.

'It can hardly have escaped your attention, My Lord,' said Jones, obviously of the opinion that Fleming was being unnecessarily obtuse, 'that the plaintiff is under cross-examination and of course, that being so, Mr Phillips, her solicitor, ought not to talk to her. It's a long-established rule and must be well known to one of Mr Phillips's experience.' Phillips was frantically trying to get Richard's attention.

'Mr Jones, are you seriously making this point?' asked Fleming.

'I wouldn't make the point at all if I wasn't making it seriously. I am, as I have said, under strict instructions.'

'What do you want me to do? Discharge the jury?'

'Precisely.'

'You can't be serious, Mr Jones? What possible grounds are there for such a course? Do you think that someone of Mr Phillips's stature might have been abusing his position as an officer of the court ... by ... by ... what? By, for example, coaching the witness? Is that what you are alleging, Mr Jones?' Fleming's tone suggested that the cord that attached Jones's application to reality had been well and truly severed.

Richard was not to be excluded. 'My Lord, if I may interrupt?'

'Of course, Mr Thornton.'

'Thank you ... that's a ... Mr Phillips instructs me ... that's a ... that the case was not discussed between himself and his client over lunch.'

'I never doubted it for a moment, Mr Thornton,' Fleming said.

'If Your Lordship would allow me to reply?'

'I do not think that will be necessary, Mr Jones. In my opinion, this application has no merit, particularly having regard to Mr Thornton's assurance that the case was not discussed. Please continue, Mr Jones.'

Jones could see no light at the end of this tunnel and so, basking in the more important success of being allowed to continue his line of cross-examination, he turned to the as-yet-unoccupied witness box. Richard renewed his invitation to Barbara who, for the second time that day, made her way up to her throne where she gave another discreet tug to her skirt, sat down and crossed her legs. Meanwhile, Fleming's crier had brought back the jury.

'Yes, Mr Jones?' Barbara said. It wasn't customary for a witness to bring the battle to her interrogator quite as bluntly as this.

'Thank you, *Miss* Sorenson.' The mutual courtesy was as sincere as Jones's smile.

'I was suggesting to you, before my friend's unsuccessful attempt to limit my cross-examination, that the column you wrote in the past for your tab ... your newspaper did not merit the title of social column and you disagreed. I went on to suggest that one of my principal reasons for this observation was that you wrote with little concern for the truth. Isn't that so?'

'Isn't what so, Mr Jones? That I wrote with little concern for the truth or that you went on to suggest that that was the principal reason for your observation?'

'Both, Miss Sorenson.'

'I did my best,' Barbara said humbly. 'It wasn't always possible to be accurate and, if I wasn't, the person I offended could always resort to the courts.'

'As they did in great numbers in your case, I think?'

Phillips passed another note to Richard who received it and added it to the skyscraper of notes that rose from the table in front of him. It was testimony to Phillips's tendency to confine himself to Fitzwilliam Square and only exceptionally take the ferry to the Four Courts.

'Great numbers is an exaggeration, Mr Jones.'

'Very well, Miss Sorenson. But they weren't uncommon, were they?'

'They weren't uncommon, Mr Jones.' Hunter and prey, they met for a moment in their consensus.

'Miss Sorenson, in your ten years writing what you euphemistically call your "social column", you did much harm. Is that not so?'

'I believe it is.'

'You damaged many reputations, would that be correct?'

'I believe it is.'

'You caused the break up of many marriages?'

'Personally?'

'By what you wrote.'

'I don't think so.'

'Were you never sued by people who claimed that their marriages ended because of what you wrote?'

'I was.'

'More than once?'

'Yes.'

I had never witnessed such drama in court. The removal of the death penalty has taken a lot of the tension out of murder cases. Personal injury litigation is the poorer for the abolition of juries. There is little left that is exciting in the law and much of that is to be found in the defamation court. This was as good as it got – giants of the Library slogging it out with Fleet Street. The courtroom, this October afternoon, was packed as tightly as Barbara's skirt. The jury, the judge, the barristers and solicitors, the journalists scribbling away, all hung on every word. If the acoustics let them down occasionally, they turned to their neighbour to make up the deficit.

'Ms Sorenson, there is a glass of water on the ledge in front of you if you would like it,' said Fleming. It was not essential for Fleming to make this intervention. Had she been in the thick of a divorce case and it was being put to her that she was an alcoholic nymphomaniac and therefore not a fit person to have custody of her two-year-old twins, it would have been understandable. Had she been the victim in a rape trial and this was the moment when counsel for the accused put to her her earlier promiscuous lifestyle, again it might have been acceptable. But, while Jones's cross-examination was no teddy-bear's picnic, Barbara was more than up to it.

'Thank you, My Lord.' Not wishing to offend the judge by refusing his invitation, she sipped water from the glass in front of her.

Jones chose not to be side-tracked. 'Don't you think, Miss Sorenson, that there is an extraordinary irony in the fact that, as one who once wrote this sort of lie for a living yourself ...'

Without any prompting from Phillips, Richard was on his feet. 'Is my friend conceding the untruth of his client's words about the witness because, if so, I would ask Your

Lordship ... that's a ... to treat the case from here on in as an assessment only ... merely a matter of damages.'

'Mr Jones?' inquired the judge.

'My friend knows well what I mean. He is being disingenuous. There is absolutely no question of my conceding anything,' said Jones.

'That will hardly come as a surprise to Mr Thornton,' Fleming said as he smiled down at Jones, who was no doubt feeling, however slightly, the exposure.

Uncharacteristically, Jones had dropped his guard. For once, he had allowed his personal opinion of the witness and her pen to intrude on the ruthless detachment of his cross-examination. 'Lest there be any doubt, I will rephrase my question,' he offered.

'I think, Mr Jones, that that might be a good idea. I did warn you of the danger of the territory,' advised Fleming. It is not often that the Bench has a chance of getting the better of Jones. He is brighter than most of them. Fleming was determined to stitch it in.

'Miss Sorenson, as I was saying. Would you agree that it is something of a monumental irony' – Jones was upping the stakes – 'that, as a person who formerly made her living out of articles more often than not both untrue and cruel, that you yourself should now be seeking damages as the victim of an observation which, albeit cruel, is, at least in the opinion of the writer, true?'

Once again, no note from Phillips in sight, Richard was on his feet. It seemed that he was more likely to rise to his feet when unprompted by Phillips. 'I am sorry to interrupt my friend again ... that's a ... but, My Lord, this question seems to contain a number of assumptions,' Richard submitted.

'I agree with Mr Thornton, My Lord,' Barbara was now quite at home with the law.

'It might be better, Ms Sorenson, if you leave the law to Mr Thornton and myself. We ... I mean Mr Thornton will make sure that you will not be at any disadvantage.' His Lordship was not quite as detached as he might have been. 'I think Mr Thornton is correct. In fact, I think it is more comment than question and therefore something for an address to the jury rather than cross-examination of this witness, though, at the rate we're going, no one will be addressing the jury for some time.'

'I'll move on, Miss Sorenson,' Jones said.

'It might be as well, Mr Jones,' Barbara added encouragingly. I doubted if any witness had ever spoken to Jones like this before.

'You will forgive me for asking this question, but I am obliged to put my client's case to you so that you can respond to it. Do you understand?' Barbara understood perfectly.

'The truth is that you did "play away from home", didn't you?' Jones continued. The court stiffened. Either she did or she did not. There were no damages for words, however hurtful, that were true.

'I am not sure that I understand you, Mr Jones.'

'Come now, Miss Sorenson. What do you mean you don't understand me? What precisely do you not understand?'

'"Playing away from home", Mr Jones. What does that mean?'

'It is a sporting analogy.'

'I am not a sporting person.'

'But, Miss Sorenson, if you do not know what the phrase means how can you claim that you were defamed by it?' Jones was back in the driving seat. Barbara hesitated.

'Ms Sorenson, when Mr Jones asks you if you had ...' Fleming's rescue operation was itself interrupted by Jones.

'With the greatest of respect, could I ask Your Lordship to allow the witness to answer the question unassisted?'

'I feel that the witness is confused, Mr Jones, and, in fairness to her, I think she should be taken out of her confusion,' Fleming said.

'She has shown no signs of confusion today, My Lord. Indeed, quite the opposite.'

'Thank you, Mr Jones.' Fleming continued the rescue operation as if there had been no interruption. 'Ms Sorenson, when Mr Jones was asking you about "playing away from home", he was referring to the words written by Mr Thompson.' There was a pause. Fleming looked at Barbara. Barbara looked at Fleming. Jones looked furious. The lifeline was about to reach Barbara at last.

'Oh, My Lord, I see. I see now what he means. The article. That I "played away from home". Of course. Now I see. How foolish of me.'

'Oh, good. Now that seems to clear the matter up. Perhaps, Mr Jones, you would like to proceed?' Fleming said, satisfied.

'I would indeed, but I think that it might be fairer to the parties if Your Lordship left the cross-examination to me and the salvage work to Mr Thornton.' Fleming had resumed his note of the evidence and was paying not the slightest attention to Jones's lecture on fairness. Jones decided to take a leaf out of the judge's book and re-focus his own attention.

'Now that we understand one another, Miss Sorenson.'

'I am sorry, Mr Jones. It was slow of me,' Barbara turned to see what impact her apology was having on the jury. They were difficult to read.

'"Away from home", Miss Sorenson?' Jones short-ened his question, perhaps in an effort to make up some time.

'Never, Mr Jones. My husband is and always has been very dear to me. I would never have done such a thing had I been minded to and I was never minded to.' Denials rarely came clearer than that. 'I am not saying that I was a saint before I married him,' she added.

'No one is asking if you were, Miss Sorenson.' Jones said, looking knowingly at the jury.

'I don't think you understand, Mr Jones. I wasn't a saint before. I'm not a saint now,' Barbara explained not altogether clearly. 'It's just that I'm not trying to claim the high moral ground. I did have liaisons before I married, but after ... never.'

'I won't trouble you with your pre-marital romances, Miss Sorenson.'

'Thank you.'

'Except to say that they were numerous ...'

'My Lord ...' interrupted my leader. But before he had a chance to say 'that's a', His Lordship accepted the cue.

'I don't think so, Mr Jones.'

'If it please Your Lordship,' complied Jones, the damage done. 'But you say that after you married your husband there was no one apart from him, is that so?'

'That is correct.'

Jones paused to allow this assertion of marital fidelity to sink in. When he felt that it had sunk in sufficiently, he continued, 'Of course, if that statement happened to be untrue you would not be entitled to damages, Miss Sorenson, isn't that so?'

'I am not here for damages. If it were merely a question of money, I would not be here at all.'

'What are you here for then, Miss Sorenson?'

'To defend my marriage, Mr Jones, and to assert its integrity in the face of this pernicious and unfounded attack by your client,' Barbara replied with passion.

'I repeat, Miss Sorenson, if that statement were untrue your case would fail, is that not so?'

'Yes.'

'The success of your case depends, Miss Sorenson, on the truth of your assertion that you have been faithful to your husband, is that not so?' Barbara nodded. She and Jones faced up to one another. Once again, he paused to allow the full significance of question and answer to sink in.

'Miss Sorenson, I wonder if you could be mistaken?' Jones was giving her a final chance.

'What do you mean, Mr Jones?' The packed court hung on every word and every pause.

'Could I take you back two summers, Miss Sorenson?'

'That's not so long ago.'

'Not so long ago indeed. To the month of August to be precise. You have told us that you're not interested in sport, but in fact I think you do play a little golf.'

'Very little and not very well, unfortunately.'

'Be that as it may, Miss Sorenson, did you not spend a week in a golfing resort called La Cala in the South of Spain?'

'I did and I highly recommend it.'

'You met a male friend while you were there, I think?'

'I met many people while I was there. I like company, Mr Jones.'

'Male company in particular, Miss Sorenson?'

'I have many female friends, Mr Jones.'

'There was one gentleman in particular, was there not?' Barbara began to look a little uncomfortable. She uncrossed her legs so as to reverse them. As she did so, her eyes scanned the court. What was coming? Having surveyed the court, she seemed to relax a little. As if to mark this recovery, she returned her legs to their original position.

'Would you mind looking at this photograph?' Jones asked as he passed a photograph to the witness via his solicitor. At the same time, Phillips passed yet another note to my leader.

'I'm sure ... that's a ... that I don't have to ... that's a ... remind my learned friend of the necessity for formally proving the photograph,' Richard said.

'I'm sure you don't, Mr Thornton,' Fleming added. 'You will be calling the photographer to prove the photograph, Mr Jones?'

'In this day and age, My Lord?' Jones asked incredulously.

'Rules of evidence, Mr Jones.'

'Not so strict surely, My Lord? This is not a nineteenth-century murder trial. Surely I don't still have to call a photographer to prove a photograph?'

Phillips was becoming excited and, on this occasion, decided on a verbal communication with his leading counsel. 'No photographer, Richard.'

'Very good, Phillips,' replied Richard, like a teacher encouraging a remedial student who had got something right.

'And will I need the negative as well, My Lord?' Jones asked facetiously, invoking an even stricter rule of evidence.

'Not if you don't have a photographer, Mr Jones,' Fleming said, terminating the exchange.

Jones decided to move on. 'Miss Sorenson, a gentleman by the name of González, Jose González, will say that he met you in La Cala and that he had a relationship with you while you were there.' As he posed this question to Barbara in a manner that belied its gravity, Jones was fingering his brief in an absentminded way, as if looking for something of no great importance. He finished the question but carried on looking at his brief. The court was still. After a few moments, when no reply was forthcoming, he looked up at Barbara who was staring down at him.

'Well, Miss Sorenson?'

'Well what, Mr Jones?'

'What do you say to that?'

'Oh, you are asking me a question. I thought you were in the middle of a statement and had not concluded.' I wasn't sure that Barbara's apparent innocence would convince the jury.

'Now that you are aware that I am asking you a question, would you like to favour the members of the jury with your reply?'

'My reply? Simple. I deny it of course, deny it entirely, for the lie, the wicked, unfounded lie it is.' Perhaps Barbara was protesting too much? 'I recall the gentleman of course ... if gentleman you can call him ... but I most certainly did not have an affair with him.'

'Mr Jones, will you be much longer with this witness?' Fleming wanted to know.

'I will, My Lord.'

'In that case, I think it might be as well to leave what's left of your cross-examination until the morning, when we will all be fitter and fresher.'

'As Your Lordship pleases.'

'The court stands adjourned until eleven o'clock tomorrow morning,' the crier announced and, with that, the first day of Sorenson *v. The Irish Daily News* came to an end, and judge and crier disappeared into the evening. The jury dispersed.

The trial was exceeding expectations. Excited conversation rippled around the courtroom. I could hear Richard muttering something about cross-examination to Phillips – presumably a reminder not to talk to Barbara – and then he was gone, back to Merrion Square and his violin. Phillips, who had repeatedly warned his team not to talk to the press, was giving interviews left, right and centre.

He was delighted with himself. Perhaps he didn't fully appreciate the significance of Jones's cross-examination. For, if Señor González turned out to be a credible witness, Barbara's case would be blown clean out of the Mediterranean. There was no sign of this realisation on Phillips's face as he ushered the photographers, who shouldn't have been in the building at all, out into the Round Hall where the light was more favourable.

'See you at ten in the morning,' Phillips shouted back to me as he disappeared from view, flanked by Barbara on one side and Amy and Sophie on the other.

'Eleven, Mr Phillips, eleven,' I corrected, but I doubted if he heard.

As I emerged from Court 4, I saw Thompson striding across the Round Hall in the direction of the quays and, perhaps, a flutter in Leopardstown.

'Great opening, Mac,' Frank shouted from the adjoining table in the restaurant. The fact that he had made a similar jibe over lunch was not going to deter him. He is one of those people who believes that humour ripens with repetition and so I could expect the same crack for another week or two at least. No one passed our table without stopping to see how Barbara had got on in the afternoon. David could understand someone wanting to give her a 'bit away from home'. Cormac, true to form, wanted to debate the correctness of insisting on the photographer in modern litigation. He was on his own. I was the centre of attention and, like Phillips, was enjoying every minute of it.

'Suppose you'll be doing the case yourself tomorrow?' Frank said, in a predictable variation on his theme.

'Not a chance, Frank. Richard is stuck in,' I replied.

'Are you sure, Mac?' Mark enquired. 'He's not the most reliable.'

'Perfectly sure. He'd have told me if there was a problem.'

We went our separate ways. There had been enough of the case and enough coffee for one day.

*

The news had no sooner ended on the telly that night when the phone rang. My mother. 'Congratulations, darling. I saw your case on the news. She'll get a fortune. You can't say that sort of thing about a religious affairs correspondent, now can you?'

I could have explained to my mother that you could if it was true, but her question was entirely rhetorical. She wasn't going to start listening to me at this hour of her life.

'Your solicitor is very impressive, Dermot. Not at all like how you have described him.' I was on the point of explaining that this was a new solicitor from Fitzwilliam Square and not Arnold from Gardiner Street, but again she wasn't listening. 'Better let you go, dear. I'm sure you have lots of preparation for tomorrow,' she said and hung up.

'Who's that, Dermot?' Rachel wanted to know.

'Just Mum getting the wrong end of the stick again.'

'Maybe so, Dermot, but at least she's interested enough to ring.'

Rachel's parents are too busy to ring. They are interested in Rachel, of course, and in her career, but it is the interest of proprietors. Rachel is a rising star in the Law Library. That much they know. It is important to them in much the same way that their recently acquired villa in Tuscany and their entry for Cheltenham is important to them. Rachel is a jewel in their crown, a crown that they have worked hard to assemble. But they do not have time to ring.

I thought I'd just flick through my notes for an hour or so and retire early. The case deserved my full attention the following day, if only in a supporting role. I had just begun when the phone rang again.

'It's Richard,' Rachel whispered as she handed me the portable.

'Is that you, Dermot?' It was Richard all right. I could hear music in the background.

'Yes, Richard. What can I do for you?'

'Quite a lot actually, Dermot.' This *was* a surprise. 'Sorry for ringing so late.' Not a 'that's a' so far. 'I'm afraid something rather urgent has come up for tomorrow and there is nothing I can do about it.' Richard paused. 'I should be with you by two. Does that present any problems for you?'

I could hardly tell him that it was my first libel action and that I had no idea what to do next. 'Not at all. Delighted,' I said.

'Excellent, Dermot. Thank you. I knew I could rely on you.'

I waited for Richard's instructions as to how to proceed the following morning. After some moments, I heard him say, 'Good night then, Dermot, and thank ...'

'Just before you go, Richard. Is there any particular approach you would like me to take?' I said quickly.

'Not really, Dermot. It's impossible to anticipate how these cases will develop. You really have to make it up as you go along.' This wasn't very helpful. He must have sensed my unease because he added, 'There's one thing I would suggest, Dermot.' My pen was ready. 'Whatever you do, keep your cross-examination short.'

'That won't be hard,' I muttered.

'You'd be surprised how many libel actions are lost by cross-examinations that go on too long.' Richard was serious. I was keen to keep him talking but I couldn't think of any more questions. 'Well, Dermot, if you have nothing else on your mind ...'

'Before you go, Richard ...' I knew there was one particular thing I wanted to ask him about but it was hiding in the back of my mind. 'What about ...'

'What about what, Dermot?'

Oh, yes.

'La Cala, Richard ... what about yer man in La Cala? How will I deal with him?'

'González? I don't know. I have a funny feeling about La Cala and González. Get an early night and if anything further occurs to you, do ring me back. I'll be at my desk for another few hours ... that's a ... good night.' There was as much chance of me ringing him back as there was of me getting an early night.

'What did Richard want, Dermot?' Rachel asked from the television room.

'He can't be there in the morning. Hopes to make it by two.'

'I could have told you.'

'Well, *he* could have told me ... earlier I mean. How do they do it, Rachel?'

'How do who do what?' asked Rachel, whose exclusive attention I obviously did not have at that moment.

'Silks, Rachel. Silks. How do they get away with it? Dropping in and out of cases like characters in a play. What about Barbara? Is she not entitled to her Senior's commitment from start to finish?'

'You'll never take silk if that's your attitude, Dermot.'

'And what about Phillips? What'll he say?'

'He doesn't matter, Dermot. Richard doesn't need Phillips. Richard doesn't need anyone.'

I put the kettle on. What else was I to do? The early night that I had intended and that was so high up on Richard's list of advice had now joined the ranks of those aspirations at the beginning of the Constitution with as little chance of implementation.

Reading my notes took on greater urgency. As the imminence of execution helps to concentrate the mind of the condemned, Richard's phone call helped to concentrate mine. Sadly, my notes left much to be desired. It wasn't easy, even sitting securely behind your Senior, to listen to the evidence and take a note. I did my best to make sense of the scratchings and doodles in the notebook in front of me.

I tried to anticipate how things might unfold the following day. I did not know how much longer Jones would be with Barbara. Then, after her, her husband would take the stand briefly. Then, on behalf of the defendant, Thompson. And, after him, presumably González. What on earth would I ask him? If he got into the box and swore that he had an affair with Barbara in La Cala, what would I do then? After all, wasn't that why Richard was in the case, to reduce the treacherous Iberian to a heap of mendacious rubble? Wasn't that why, to put it crudely, he was paid fifty per cent more than his Junior, Dermot McNamara?

I prepared my cross-examination of Thompson and González by writing out a series of questions. When these filled a few pages, I re-read them, thought of Richard's advice about not going on too long and started again. It was about two when I woke up on the sofa. Django Reinhardt, who I had playing in the background, had given up on me. I took myself off to bed where Rachel was sleeping soundly.

*

I was tired when I woke the next morning. For a few moments I was protected from the realisation of what lay ahead. Then, all of a sudden, a host of butterflies invaded my stomach. As I shaved and showered, I rehearsed my cross-examination. Why is it that the questions crafted at midnight, so compelling then, lose their conviction in the light of dawn? Over breakfast, the pages of preparation were whittled down so that, by default rather than design, Richard's advice to keep cross-examination to a minimum would be complied with. Thoughtfully, Rachel rose to the moment and delivered our darlings to school.

The Law Library is a busy place. It is especially so at around ten in the morning. Solicitors arrive and call their barristers. Consultations take place. Barristers try to work out the logistics of the day ahead, wondering how to juggle the briefs that they have accumulated for the same time in different courts. This leads to last-minute handovers. Solicitors are left to explain to perplexed clients how the balding barrister at the consultation the evening before has become overnight a youthful barrister with a pony tail. Of course, the solicitor explains, the new man will do an even better job.

The Library can be a lonely place too. Indeed, the busier it is, the lonelier it is, if you are not busy also. Every barrister knows that because every barrister has been there. An empty pigeonhole, a day not in court is enough to stir the insecurities of even the most successful barrister.

For this morning at least, the insecurity of life at the Bar was not my problem. Today, the pressure was different. I was alone all right, but in a different sense. I was without my leader on the second day of a trial that was making the nation's headlines. *The Irish Times* may not have had it on its front page, but it had it nonetheless. And it was the story that was selling the other newspapers for the day. This did nothing to calm the butterflies in my stomach, which were fast coming to the conclusion that they had been better off as caterpillars. I double-checked my wig and gown and that my tabs were in place, and headed for Phillips in the Round Hall.

'Where on earth is Richard?' Phillips quizzed me immediately, as if in some way I was responsible for the whereabouts of our leader. 'I have been looking for him everywhere.' Apparently, though perhaps not surprisingly, Richard hadn't contacted Phillips.

'We won't see him until two,' I announced as calmly as the butterflies allowed. 'At the earliest,' I added.

'What? Two?' Phillips replied, as if the repetition might alter the de facto situation.

'Yes, two.'

The Round Hall was crowded, with most of the interest centred on Court 4, the high altar of defamation litigation.

'He won't be here until two?' Barbara appeared beside me in a striking new outfit. 'This is very inconvenient, a complete waste of a morning.'

'What do you mean, Ms Sorenson?' I asked.

'Well, I assume we'll have to go away and re-assemble at two o'clock.' She noticed that this assumption was not greeted immediately with confirmation and so added, 'Won't we?' Apparently her worst fears had yet to be confirmed.

'I'm afraid it doesn't work like that, Ms Sorenson. The judge waits for no man, not even Mr Thornton. The show must go on,' I enlightened her.

'This isn't a show, Dermot. This is my life, my reputation, my marriage,' Barbara pleaded as if to the jury, which at that moment was gathering in the jury room. 'Am I not entitled to be represented?' she appealed to her Junior Counsel, her solicitor and his two still-apprentices.

'This is precisely why you have two counsel, Barbara,' Phillips reassured her. 'This is why Dermot is here. To step into the breach.'

'But there shouldn't be a breach, should there? Mr Thornton should be here.' She paused and then added in an instruction that indicated less than total confidence in me, 'The case will have to be adjourned until he gets back.'

I was becoming increasingly irritated by this distraction from the task ahead, not to mention the not-very-subtle aspersions Barbara was casting on my competence.

'The judge will not adjourn your case for a reason as insubstantial as Mr Thornton's absence, Ms Sorenson,' I announced in an effort to stamp my authority on the discussion and convey my annoyance at the same time.

'Dermot is right, Barbara,' said Phillips. 'Such an application will not do your case any good. In any event, Dermot is very highly thought of in this area and is well up to the job.' Good for Phillips. There are times when the whole truth is not called for. Our two apprentices, who looked as if they didn't have much time for either study or sleep the night before, were nodding their pretty heads.

This exchange was brought to an end by the intervention of the judge's pleasant crier who informed us that his boss was about to sit. No matter how ill-equipped Barbara felt I was for the task ahead, my duty then as a barrister was to be in court when the judge sat. Accordingly, I turned on my heels and followed the crier into the chamber of defamation.

The room was already full. Barbara and her husband took their places. There was no sign of Thompson. If it wasn't for my wig and gown I would never have been able to burrow my way through to the bench reserved for Junior Counsel. Others in court had the luxury of being spectators and could sit back and enjoy the unfolding plot. I was not sure if one of Jones's experience had such a luxury, but I certainly did not. There was no one between me and the Bench, no one to intercept the judicial arrows, no one to ask the incisive questions of the witness, who was clearly telling whoppers. What was I to do or say when His Lordship turned to me and said, 'Your witness, Mr McNamara.' I was about to find out.

'All rise!' Out ran the crier. Out ran the judge. This was an enthusiastic team, well rested and eager to get at the evidence. The wise seat was drawn back by the crier so that Fleming could be settled therein with minimum fuss and maximum dignity. With or without Richard, the show would indeed go on.

'Are we not to have the pleasure of your leaders, gentlemen?' Fleming enquired of the two Junior Counsel in the case. Until that moment, I was so taken up with Richard's absence that I did not notice that Jones was not in court either. My spirits momentarily soared. Perhaps my opposite number would look for time. He rose to his feet.

'Mr Jones has asked me to request Your Lordship to rise for a moment,' my opposite number informed Fleming.

Fleming acceded to the application and was about to make for his room when a noise at the back of the court signalled Jones's arrival. I looked around. As Jones was making his way through the crowd of people standing at the edge of the court, Thompson, in a proud new bow-tie, was taking his reserved place.

'As precise as ever, Mr Jones ... or almost anyway,' Fleming said, as Jones, with a deep bow to the judicial icon above, began settling himself in front of his relieved Junior.

'May it please Your Lordship,' he said, which was as close as Jones could get to an apology.

Fleming turned his attention to me. 'Mr McNamara, would you like me to rise for a moment? More than likely your leader is caught in traffic.' This was kind of Fleming, particularly as it was a well-known fact that Richard didn't drive. I was on the point of asking the judge to rise until two, thereby keeping my client happy, but such an application wasn't appropriate. I was present and in possession of all my faculties. What possible justification could there be for such an application?

'Thank you, My Lord, but we are ready to go on,' I informed Fleming stoutly.

'Well, in that case, gentlemen, let's get on with it.'

This was about as close as a barrister could get to the coalface. I may not have been in danger of contracting pneumoconiosis, but at least there was no doubt that my career was well and truly on the line. By lunch hour, if the gods looked unkindly on me, I could be looking up FÁS courses. It was with trepidation that I contemplated the hours that lay ahead.

'Mr Jones, you were cross-examining Ms Sorenson when we left off yesterday afternoon. Perhaps you would like to resume,' continued Fleming.

Jones rose to his feet as Barbara once again made her way through the courtroom to the witness box, where she had been so comfortable the day before. I got my pen ready for the day's nuggets.

'Good morning, Ms Sorenson,' Fleming greeted her warmly as she settled in her seat. Clearly there had been no reduction in the judge's testosterone levels since the day before. 'Mr Jones has a few further questions I think.'

'Thank you, My Lord,' Barbara said, apparently still enjoying Fleming's attention. The grimace on Jones's face signalled his fury at this cosiness. If Barbara had any apprehension about what lay ahead, she did not show it. The courtroom was full of silent expectation.

'My Lord.'

'Yes, Mr Jones?' Fleming responded.

Jones paused. He seemed to be having difficulty. 'My Lord,' he repeated. Something was bothering him. 'I have no further questions for this witness,' he said at last, almost inaudibly, and sat down.

I could not believe what I was hearing. This was a development that I had not anticipated. The one certainty from the previous day was the continuation of Jones's cross-examination of Sorenson and that it should not be missed. And now – no further questions. I looked over at Jones; he was as inscrutable as ever.

Fleming looked down at Jones, whose gaze was fixed firmly on his clenched hands on the table in front of him. Fleming turned to me but I was of no assistance to him either. Of course, I realised that a highly significant development had taken place in the case and one that was undoubtedly beneficial to my client, but I hadn't fully grasped it. Happily, Fleming chose not to pursue the development with me at that moment.

'Mr Jones, yesterday afternoon, if I recall correctly, you put to Barbara ... I mean to Ms Sorenson that she had an affair with Mr González in La Cala, is that not so?'

'It is, My Lord.' It was perfectly clear that Jones did not wish to be drawn into any protracted discussion of the development that had just taken place. It was equally clear that Fleming was hell bent on precisely that. Whether this was from a desire to conduct the case in a proper manner or to heighten Jones's discomfort would be a talking point for some time to come.

'And, further, I understood that this was the cornerstone of your defence to this action, is that not so?' His Lordship continued.

'It is,' Jones answered quietly.

'Well, Mr Jones?'

'My Lord?'

'What is the jury to make now of this allegation by your client against the plaintiff?' Fleming asked in a tone that suggested to the jury and everyone else that he too did not know what to make of the turn of events.

'It is quite simple, as Your Lordship well knows,' Jones replied impatiently, unimpressed by Fleming's pretence at being at forensic sea. 'I put the allegation to the plaintiff. She answered it. I have no further questions of this witness.' As Jones answered each question from the Bench he resumed his seat, hoping by the gesture to draw a line in the sand and encourage the Bench to move on. The Bench, however, was not so inclined.

'The fact that you are not pursuing the matter, Mr Jones, has implications of a fundamental nature for the defence of the action, is that not so?' Fleming asked.

'It is,' Jones conceded, on this occasion hardly rising from his seat.

Fleming felt that those implications should be spelt out. 'I will have to inform the jury that you – and therefore your client – are bound by Ms Sorenson's answer to your questions.'

'My Lord,' Jones muttered.

'And, accordingly, the position is that Ms Sorenson did not have an affair with Mr González.'

'My Lord.'

'And that, in the absence of further evidence, she has indeed been defamed by the words written.' Jones neither rose nor spoke. He had tired of conceding. Fleming must have realised that he had gone as far as he could with him. He turned to me. I had been listening very closely to the exchange between the two and was very grateful to Fleming for illuminating matters.

'May it please Your Lordship,' I responded formally, with a new found confidence. But the judge had a little more in mind.

'Mr McNamara, where do we go from here?' Precisely my own thoughts but I could hardly say that. Only the judge is allowed to declare his helplessness. However, he must have sensed my need for direction. 'Have you any more witnesses, Mr McNamara?' he enquired. Of course, witnesses. Had I any more witnesses? I looked at Phillips.

'What about Mr Kennedy?' Amy whispered. *Of course, Mr Kennedy. Barbara's husband. Thank you, Amy.*

'Thank you, My Lord.' I summoned Mr Kennedy.

I stumbled Barbara's husband through his evidence, which Jones left unchallenged. While I had the impression that he was not as elderly as he made out and that the article had not had quite as catastrophic an effect on his marriage as was claimed, at the end of his evidence Barbara's hurt remained intact.

It was midday and, before I had time to consider my next move, Fleming, to my immense relief, announced that he had to give judgment in another case and that, as it would take a little time, it might be as well to adjourn until two o'clock.

'Well done, Dermot,' Barbara said when we reassembled in the Round Hall. 'I should never have doubted you.' I was on the point of saying that I had done nothing when it occurred to me that, while I may not have been responsible for bringing about these major developments in the case, I had at least been there, minding the fort as it were, when they unfolded. Accordingly, I decided that Barbara was right and that I was entitled to at least some of the credit for what happened. I thanked her for the compliment which, I was pleased, had been overheard by Phillips.

Although I had not formally closed my case and therefore Jones was not to know that I was not calling any more witnesses, we knew that our evidence was over and that it was now up to the defendant to do his best. As we were talking, I could see Jones having a serious word with Thompson. Obviously it had been some last-minute instructions, presumably about González, that had kept the two of them late for court earlier in the day. Then Thompson turned around and, less confidently than the day before, made his way across the Round Hall and out into the lunchtime traffic.

'Barbara, what about lunch?' Phillips invited, taking advantage of being free again to talk to his client. 'Now that we have an extra hour maybe we'll try the prawns provençal in the Lord Edward. I'm sure Dermot will appreciate a bit more time to prepare for the afternoon.' Richard seemed to have been forgotten.

'Richard hopes to join us at two,' I reminded them.

'Once the sun disappears it rarely returns,' Phillips said philosophically, as he and the three ladies headed for the hill.

Neither prawns provençal nor any other kind of prawns were on our downstairs menu that day. However, the bangers and chips tasted better than ever.

'What next, Mac?' Mark wanted to know as he peeled his banana.

'I suppose Thompson will give evidence,' I said.

'What about?' Cormac chipped in. 'You say the justification is gone.'

'It is, well and truly. Fleming made that abundantly clear. Really all the defence can do now is make out that she doesn't have a reputation,' I said.

'Having regard to the rubbish she used to write in her previous life, it mightn't be a bad plan B,' Cormac commented.

'Precisely,' I agreed. 'And no better person than Thompson to give that evidence.'

'Anyway, that's not your problem now,' Afric added supportively. 'Time for Thornton to earn his fee.'

'If he turns up,' Mark said.

'He said he'd be free at two,' I said. 'It's almost that now. I'd better go back.'

'Good luck either way, Mac,' Afric shouted after me.

It was five to two and there was still no sign of Richard. The prawns-provençal four were back. Uncharted waters lay ahead. I would have been quite happy to return the limelight to my leader and live on the memory of the morning. Jones was not one to lie down easily and, as surely as the Four Courts were designed by Mr Gandon, he was going to come out of his corner fighting this afternoon. The friendly crier informed us that it was time to take our seats and so we went in. The vacuum before me loomed as large as ever. However, Seniors are known for their timing and I had not yet given up on Richard.

All of a sudden the door of the chambers opened and the judge came out onto the bench of Court 4 for the second time that day.

'Sorenson *v. The Irish Daily News*,' the registrar announced.

'Well, Mr McNamara,' Fleming said.

'May it please Your Lordship,' I responded with as much gravitas as my recently acquired expertise in libel actions allowed me to muster. 'That's the plaintiff's case, My Lord,' I announced with deliberation, hoping that I had left nothing out. This was a moment of no return. Evidence not adduced at this point remained so with whatever consequences. His Lordship did not seem at all surprised by this announcement and from that I took encouragement.

'Thank you, Mr McNamara, and, if I may say so, a job well done,' he said. I found it difficult to conceal my pleasure at this judicial endorsement.

'Mr Jones, over to you,' Fleming said.

This was what the crowd had assembled for this afternoon. Jones, who had been having a bad day at the office, would fight back. Of that there was no doubt. He was not a leader of the Bar for nothing. I still had a concern that his opening words might be the forensic equivalent of 'gotcha', that I had left something out and that he would pounce on the omission. He rose slowly.

'My Lord,' he said quietly. The entire courtroom strained to hear. The more the courtroom strained, the quieter Jones's voice became. 'I will not be going into evidence,' he said softly and resumed the seat which, once again, had not expected him back so soon.

For the second time that day I could not believe what I was hearing. From the heady heights of the previous afternoon when Jones first raised Barbara's romance in the south of Spain, Jones's case had plummeted to this announcement that there would not be a word from the defendant. I looked around. There was a big smile on Barbara's face. Thompson's head was in his hands.

The initial surprise on the part of those present gave way to curiosity as to what might happen next, a curiosity that was shared by the judge. 'Where does that leave us?' he wanted to know. I had no idea – things were happening a bit fast – so I thought I would take a leaf out of Jones's book and keep my head as far down as I could without my wig falling off.

'The questions, I suppose,' I heard Jones answer in a voice tired of Fleming's cries for assistance.

I have often heard it said that what distinguishes practice in the superior courts from the lower courts is the speed at which things happen in the superior courts and, consequently, what distinguishes Senior from Junior Counsel is the ability to react to the faster pace of proceedings. It may not be true of every case, but certainly

I was getting a very strong taste of it on the second day of Ms Sorenson's libel action.

The questions were designed to assist the jury in reaching a verdict and were prepared by the judge with the assistance of counsel.

Fleming had a suggestion. 'Gentlemen, perhaps you would discuss the questions between you? I have a short matter to attend to and it may be that you could use the time wisely. Say, twenty minutes.' And he was gone. A cigarette, a crossword, a telephone call ... who knew?

Barbara wanted to know what this was all about.

'A legal matter, Barbara,' Phillips reassured her. 'Nothing that you need concern yourself with.'

I had a brief word with Jones and, to everyone's surprise, we were back in court within the allotted time. The questions were only a distraction as far as I was concerned. Richard still had not turned up. I would have to make the closing speech to the jury. This was the most important part of the case and the preserve of Senior Counsel. I hadn't given it a thought. Not for a moment did I think that it would have anything to do with me.

I was doing my best to jot down something to say to the jury, without much success. I had a strong feeling that exemplary damages came into it somewhere without quite knowing how or where. There wasn't any point in looking to Phillips. I was on my own. Time, like Richard Thornton, was not on my side.

A flurry of activity up front meant Fleming was back.

'Well, gentlemen, have you managed to agree the questions?' Fleming wanted to know.

'We have, My Lord,' I told him.

'And what are they?' I read them out to him and assumed from his response that he could not improve on them.

'Now then, the closing speeches. Best get on with them,' he encouraged and went silent. I resumed my

preparation, leaving Jones to get on with his speech to the
jury. After a silence, I looked up from my notes only to see
Jones stuck to his seat and staring in front of him.
Everyone else was staring at me.

'Mr McNamara?'

'Yes, My Lord?'

'The jury awaits your words of wisdom.' This came as
a surprise. Fleming was obviously getting the order wrong.

'Em ...' I said. 'That's a ...' I threw in for good measure.
'Em ...' I said again, 'Mr Jones first, My Lord?'

'Normally, yes, Mr McNamara. But Mr Jones has not
gone into evidence. He is entitled to the last word.' I hadn't
heard this since lectures in Kings Inns. 'Not counting me,
of course,' Fleming added. Gradually, this rule dawned on
me with the clarity of the night after exams.

'Of course,' I agreed respectfully. Without the benefit of
further ado, I was obliged to put shape on the gormless
things that were running around inside my brain. I stood up.

'That's a ...' I heard from behind. I couldn't believe it.

'Mr Thornton, how good of you to join us,' said Fleming.

'Thank you, My Lord ... that's a ...'

'We have made considerable progress in your absence,
Mr Thornton.'

'My Lord?'

'Not that I connect the two.'

'Of course not, My Lord ... that's a ... I never ...'

'Mr McNamara is about to deliver the closing speech to
the jury,' Fleming informed my leader.

'That's a ...' was all I heard from Richard as he rounded
the bend and again filled the void in front of me. I took my
cue and my seat, hoping that, as I faded from His
Lordship's sight, I might fade from his mind also. It wasn't
going to be that easy.

'As soon as you've settled in, Mr Thornton, we can let
Mr McNamara get on with it,' Fleming continued.

My heart sank. Hadn't I done enough? I thought to myself. Wasn't it time for Richard to do something? Obviously the same thought was running through his mind.

'No, My Lord ... that's a ... I will be closing the case,' Richard announced with considerable authority. A chill ran through the courtroom.

'I think not, Mr Thornton. You know my rules. You opened, Mr McNamara closes.'

'With the greatest of respect ... that's a ... how Mr McNamara and I decide to run our client's case is a matter for us ... that's a ... indeed, as the leader in the case, it is a matter for me ... that's a ... it is for me to decide who should open the case and who should close it. Your Lordship has no role in the matter,' Richard insisted.

'But you weren't even here, Mr Thornton. How can you close the case to the jury when you weren't even here?' Fleming was not lying down.

'You've gone too far, My Lord ... that's a .... Your criticisms ... that's a, in particular your last one, should not have been made in front of the jury. I must ask Your Lordship to withdraw your remarks or, alternatively, to discharge the jury.'

'I will do no such thing. What I will do, in an effort to move matters along, I will depart from my normal practice and allow you to close to the jury,' the judge said in a significant climb-down, perhaps sensing that he had in fact gone too far.

'I will close my client's case to the jury ... that's a ... as my right and not by Your Lordship's leave ... that's a ...' Richard was not to be dictated to, even by such a senior judge.

'How you choose to regard it is a matter for you, Mr Thornton. As far as I am concerned, I am allowing you to close your case. Now, perhaps if we could get on with the proceedings?'

Before addressing the jury, Richard turned to me. 'What happened in La Cala?'

'Nothing. Collapsed. No affair. No González. No evidence.'

'Exactly as I suspected ... that's a ... well done for keeping it out.' He turned his substantial frame towards the jury. There wasn't time to tell him that I hadn't kept it out and, if there had been, I wasn't going to tell him anyway. There had to be some advantage to being here all the time. The jury held its breath.

'Ladies and gentlemen of the jury, you have been listening attentively to this case for the last two days ... that's a ...' Richard placed his foot on the seat of the front bench and his hands on his thigh, one on top of the other, '... unlike myself unfortunately ... that's a ...' He was totally at ease, his row with Fleming behind him. He could have been playing his violin in his apartment.

'I can assure you of two things ... that's a ...' He spoke quietly. It didn't matter to him whether the judge or anyone else in the courtroom heard what he had to say as long as each member of the jury heard every chosen word. 'Only a matter of the gravest importance ... that's a ... would have kept me away from Barbara Sorenson's case for the better part of today.' It was as if he and his jury were alone in a sitting-room and he was sharing an interesting story with them. 'For that unavoidable absence I apologise to you and Ms Sorenson ... that's a ...' From time to time he rested his head on each shoulder. 'The second thing I would like to assure you of ... that's a ...'

It was a class act and I was privileged not just to witness it but to be on his team. It was as if he had been in court for every second of the case and had spent the night before preparing his closing speech. This was where Rachel felt ready to go – or at least where His Lordship on the bench felt she was ready to go – and maybe she was.

I wasn't, that was for sure, though I wasn't going to tell Rachel that.

'A grave duty may have taken me away from the case today, but this would not have been possible were it not for the total confidence I had in my Junior Counsel, Dermot McNamara, in whose youthful but experienced charge I left our client's case ... that's a ...' I couldn't believe what I was hearing. I stared at the blank page of the notebook in front of me. 'My confidence in him ... that's a ... was fully borne out ...' Perhaps I was being unduly modest. Perhaps I was ready to take silk.

'Let us for a moment examine what has happened ... that's a ... When we broke up yesterday afternoon, you had heard compelling evidence from Ms Sorenson about the distress she had been caused by Mr Thompson's article, the vulgarity of which was in stark contrast to her own elegant dignity ... that's a ... Just before four o'clock you heard the Law Library's leading libel lawyer' – here Richard pointed to a subdued Jones – 'put to her in cross-examination what was the core of his defence, namely that she had an affair in the south of Spain with a Spanish gentleman by the name of ... that's a ... González. I don't have to spell it out to you. If this was true, it would have been the end of Ms Sorenson's case. Overnight, at least, we had a contest.' Richard paused. 'Now, let us examine what has happened ... that's a ... during my enforced absence.'

Not once did Richard raise his voice. He barely moved as he addressed the jury. His foot remained on the seat, his hands on his outstretched thigh. Most of the time there was an enigmatic smile on his face.

'In a matter of a morning, the edifice that Mr Jones sought to construct yesterday afternoon has come tumbling down, without as much as a peep out of the defendant. Mr Thompson, the lonely figure sitting at the back of the court, the person responsible for these cruel words, doesn't even have the courage to get into the witness box.'

Richard paused again. 'Ladies and gentlemen ... above all, these courts seek truth, seek to uncover untruth no matter how skilfully disguised. The fabrication, the ... the lie ... that's a ... of Mr Thompson's article has been exposed, with the result that the defence to this action is now in shreds on the floor, where the article itself should have been before the ink was dry.' Richard was in full flight. The case, the jury and the entire courtroom were in the palm of his hand. The fact that he had been missing for most of the day was history.

'In this country we are free to write what we want, but if what we write is untrue, there is a cost and you will decide that cost for the defendant in this case. Having heard and seen Ms Sorenson in the witness box you will decide how much money the defendant should pay to her to make up to her for having untruthfully alleged that she, a married woman, slept with another man. That, members of the jury, in a nutshell is your job this afternoon ... that's a ... and I am happy to leave Barbara Sorenson, the plaintiff in this case, in your generous hands.'

As effortlessly as the sun goes down, so Richard resumed his seat. He had spoken for twenty minutes. Not a word was wasted. Not a word that wouldn't cost the defendant thousands of pounds. There wasn't a person in the courtroom who would not have wished him to go on for another twenty. Except, of course, his opposite number to whom he had left the unenviable task of replying.

Jones did his job well, taking even less time to try and restore some balance to the case. Undoubtedly, had the jury retired on the back of Richard's address, the damages would have been stratospheric. There are advantages to not calling evidence. Notwithstanding the strength of Jones's speech to the jury, this was Richard's day. If

Jones could stop Richard touching down under the posts, it would be as much as he could hope for. Every yard closer to the touchline was a bonus, as far as Jones was concerned.

The judge did not charge the jury for long. Crucially, he gave judicial confirmation to what Richard had told them, namely that the case was now an assessment only. The words written were untrue and it was for the members of the jury to assess the extent of the plaintiff's hurt and the measure of the compensation to which she was entitled.

'Ladies and gentlemen of the jury, the case is now yours and yours alone,' Fleming said. 'If I can be of any further assistance to you in the course of your deliberations, do not hesitate to inform me and I will do the best I can to resolve the problem. And now, if you would like to retire to your room and consider your verdict?'

The judge's crier conducted the jury to its room. As soon as he returned, he led Fleming to his chambers.

For the time being, we were free of judge and jury. Fleming could get back to his crossword. The jury had its job to do. I fancied a coffee. Everyone wanted to congratulate Thornton on his speech. Off-stage he was shy and retiring. He thanked the well-wishers for their well wishes and slipped out a side-door of the courtroom, which was rarely used. Those behind talked excitedly about the afternoon's proceedings and anticipated the result. Barbara was effusive in her gratitude to me and I went for coffee on a high note.

'Sit down and keep the table,' Mark said. 'I'll buy. Rombutts, I suppose?'

'Just the job,' I replied.

'Did you close as well, Mac?' Frank, who never gave up, wanted to know from the adjoining table.

'All but,' Mark chipped in as he returned with the coffee. He turned to me. 'Congratulations. Praise indeed coming from the Great One.'

'Thanks, Mark, but he was only endearing himself to the jury. He didn't mean a word of it.'

'Rubbish,' Afric interjected. 'Thornton doesn't go in for flattery. You can be well pleased with your day's work.'

'How long will they be do you think?' Mark asked me, referring to the jury's deliberations.

'An hour or so, I suppose,' I replied.

'What about Thornton? Will he wait?' Mark asked.

'Of course. He's hardly going to disappear at this stage,' Afric said.

'But he's never in the Library after four.'

'Surely if a jury is out ...' I said.

We would find out soon enough. Earlier than I expected, the crier popped his head around the restaurant door to say the jury was back. I grabbed my wig and gown, the good luck wishes of my friends and followed him out.

To my relief, Richard was there, filling his share of the front bench. I felt confident enough now to ask him, 'How much do you think they'll give, Richard?'

'Well, Dermot, I've got it wrong so often that I don't allow myself to predict anymore. Do what I can at the time and then let go. The verdict is for them and my prediction cannot affect it. What about you?'

'I have to say I'm optimistic. After your closing speech, Richard, I cannot see them being mean.'

The jury began to file back. Word had trickled through that they had reached a decision. They weren't just back for assistance. If they looked at you, they were with you. If they avoided you, they were against. I tried to engage them. I thought I got a look but wasn't sure.

'Thank you, Dermot,' Richard replied. 'Let's hope you're right. And, incidentally, what I said to the jury about your part in this ... that's a ... I meant it.' He turned around. *Wow.* I thanked his back.

Normally, by five o'clock the cleaning ladies have taken possession of the Round Hall and there isn't a barrister to be seen. But today Court 4 was humming. The case had generated much public interest over the two days and so there were hordes of journalists. Barristers not involved in the case had stayed behind, some still in their wigs and gowns. Interested members of the public, some of whom were possibly coming in after a day at the nearby zoo, crowded into the noisy courtroom. Fleming took charge.

'Well, ladies and gentlemen, have you reached a verdict?' asked Fleming. The foreman passed the jury paper to him. Fleming kept us in suspense for a few moments.

'Indeed you have,' he announced, with a broad grin on his face. 'You have found that the words written about the plaintiff are defamatory and untrue and that, in maintaining the truth of the allegation until this morning, the defendant has aggravated the injury to the plaintiff. You have awarded Ms Barbara Sorenson the sum of one hundred thousand pounds for general damages and fifty thousand pounds for exemplary damages, a grand total of one hundred and fifty thousand pounds. Thank you, ladies and gentlemen, for your patient attention to this interesting case.' He added indiscreetly, 'I have no doubt you have done the right thing. I am happy to inform you that I can release you from jury service for the next five years. You are free to go.'

As the members of the jury made their way out of the courtroom for the last time, Richard rose to his feet and asked for and was awarded judgment in that sum against the defendant. 'And costs, My Lord?'

'And costs, Mr Thornton. And my congratulations.'

'May it please Your Lordship.' Richard bowed and resumed his seat. A ceasefire had fallen on the hostilities.

'Thank you very much everyone,' Fleming said, stealing a last glance at the vindicated plaintiff as he left the bench, the final words of his crossword beckoning.

'The court stands adjourned,' the crier cried.

To Richard's enormous discomfort, before Fleming had reached his chambers, Barbara was on her tiptoes planting her lipstick on his embarrassment. 'Thank you, Richard. Thank you very much. And you, Dermot. You did a splendid job. And Phillips, thank you also, and Amy and Sophie.' There were congratulations all round.

'I would like you all to join me for dinner.' Barbara's invitation was met with a chorus of acceptance. 'Well, that's decided then,' she said. 'Let's say if we meet at seven thirty at the Lord Edward. And Richard, what about Richard? I would so like him to join us.'

As we looked around the emptying courtroom, we saw the unmistakable figure, head slightly favouring the left shoulder, depart the scene of his great victory in favour of his armchair and his violin in Merrion Square.

A NIGHT AT THE INNS

Few people relish winter. The longer the winter, the less it is relished. Hence the need for celebration. Our forebears were well aware of this. In times past they had Samhain and then, two centuries ago, Dickens invented Christmas. From the beginning of October to 25 December is far too long for barristers, and so they invented 'benchings'.

Benchings are the occasions when newly elected benchers are launched on an unsuspecting and largely indifferent world. Benchers are either elected from the ranks of the Bar or have the honour conferred upon them by virtue of their appointment to the Superior Courts. Traditionally, benchers are male, the reason for this being that there are not many female barristers and fewer female judges. Why there are not many female barristers is a matter for historians and sociologists. Why there are not more female benchers is a matter for the benchers themselves.

It is not at all clear what benchers do. Obviously they continue their full-time jobs as barristers and judges and, from this, it may be inferred that whatever they do is done on a part-time basis. It is widely believed that they run King's Inns and are responsible for the education of barristers, but it is also widely believed that all of this is done by the under treasurer in the mysterious absence of the treasurer. Nor is it clear what they are looking for when the time comes to elect a new bencher and they cast their eyes over the congregation of barristers from which they must make their choice. The evidence suggests that life is a prerequisite and death a contraindication; while being dead does not rule out the possibility of nomination, there is no known case of a deceased barrister being elected.

At the commencement of each term, the benchers, abhorring a vacuum, meet to replace the casualties of the previous term. From time to time one hears criticism of a system of election whereby a body elects its own members. However, it is a system that has served the Vatican well for many centuries, and of course golf clubs, albeit for a shorter period. Having replenished their ranks, the benchers embark on the more onerous duty of *benching* the new bencher. This involves a dinner in King's Inns at which the new bencher is the guest of honour. One can readily see how any other duties that the benchers might have would be delegated to the under treasurer.

The benchers throw themselves into the task of entertaining the new bencher-on-the-block with considerable enthusiasm. Formerly, these dinners took place on a Monday night, not a night traditionally associated with celebration. Nonetheless, benchers and Bar rallied, with the result that very often court lists for the remainder of the week had to be abandoned. Coming into more accountable times, the benchers felt that it might be more appropriate to shift the festivities to the other end of the week. In this way, only the home lives of Bar and Bench have to be sacrificed.

*

I was having a good term. A slow start for Arnold in the case of the professor against Trinity, but then a few good wins and, of course, the Sorenson case for Phillips. Ted O'Donnell's benching was coming at a good time: midterm, mid-November. Ted was a popular appointment to the High Court and it was bound to be a good night. My practice had expanded in the previous twelve months and that meant, unfortunately, an increase in the volume of paperwork. Accordingly, had my priorities been right, my sights would have been set on not having too late a night in the Inns and a weekend at the desk. However, I did feel that things had been going well and I was entitled to a small celebration myself.

Rachel was at a family law conference in Athlone and was unable to join us. Kate and Conor were with my parents. I had arranged to meet my fellow diners for an aperitif in the bar downstairs. A number of aperitifs later, we made our way up Church Street to the Inns.

King's Inns is another of Mr Gandon's masterpieces, although for some reason I always feel that he must have been away the weekend they put it up. They seem to have erected it back to front. An elegant driveway leads you to what is not immediately recognisable as a main entrance. How disappointed people must have been in times past when, upon disembarking from their carriages, they were confronted with what passes for the hall door. In driving rain and behind time we made our way through the garden that stretched out in a soaked fan before the building.

Years of experience has taught the caterers to collect the price of the dinner in advance. Benchers, of course, dine free. So they should, as they do not have the freedom to choose who they sit beside. To pay, I joined the tail-end of a queue that might have been more at home in a DART station than in this elegant eighteenth-century mansion. I barely had time to grab the last moth-eaten and ill-fitting gown, run up the steps past *The Trial of Roger Casement* and take my place.

If Viennese waltzes were popular on the north side of the city in Mr Gandon's time, then the dining hall of King's

Inns must have been the Olympic Ballroom of its day. It is a room of grandeur, as high as it is long, and its length would not give you much change out of a football pitch. Certainly, when Ted presented himself at the western end of the hall, with a view to leading the procession of benchers to the raised table at the other end, it must have been a daunting panorama that stretched out before him. Such was his popularity that the benchers turned out in numbers. Indeed, even some thought to be no longer with us defied the sceptics. Not to be found wanting, the Bar too was strongly represented so that we had a full house.

The parade began. Ted bowed to the Bar and the Bar bowed back. The Bar bowed to the benchers and the benchers bowed in return. With all the bowing, progress was slow, but then there was no hurry. The new bencher, not being used to such homage, proceeded bashfully, but, if experience was anything to go by, the adaptation process would be short, and in no time at all he would be making the journey to the benchers' table as if this was something he had been born into. Eventually, all the benchers had passed us by and we could take our own seats.

Meanwhile, at the top table, a little more time was required as benchers jostled for position, either seeking exaltation or suddenly overtaken by a sense of panic at the realisation of who might be beside them if they did not take the seating arrangements into their own hands.

'*Benedictus benedicat,*' the Chief Steward Mr Kilkelly announced from the top of the room. This was the signal to the benchers to bring their jostling to a close and, whether pleased with their level of exaltation or not, to sit down and get on with it. The signal was contagious and so we all sat down and resumed the consumption of alcohol that had been interrupted while we travelled along Church Street. The aperitifs were mingling nicely with that sensation of pleasure that arrives on a Friday afternoon and, between the two, I felt that I was on the threshold of a good evening.

I was luckier than most of the benchers in that I had Mark on my right and Afric on my left. I had a soft spot for Afric since I first saw her at the Inns though, as I was a year behind her, she didn't pay much attention to me then. It was really only in the Library that we became friendly and, of course, she is a member of our lunch table.

Across from me sat Laurence, heavy and heavy going. Laurence takes himself and his wine equally seriously, and at this moment was studying the wine list with an intensity normally reserved for a brief in those final moments before the Supreme Court sits. He proclaimed himself satisfied with the selection of wines on offer courtesy of the wine committee of King's Inns, one of the more popular committees, but not without bemoaning the fact that the cellar's flagships were reserved for the top table.

'Don't worry, Laurence. You'll be up there yourself one day,' Jimmy reassured him. Jimmy trades on his working-class background. He had been a radical at college and spent much of his time debating reform of the legal profession. Ten years on, he hasn't changed much. He hates the trappings of being a barrister. Dinners in the Inns and bowing to benchers are high up his list of trappings. He was only at Ted's benching because he fancied Sonia, his current devil, who was sitting beside him.

'For God's sake, let's not have any more of that Chablis stuff, no matter what the cru is,' I roared across the table at Laurence, in an attempt to influence selection. Laurence was not going to heed me on much and certainly not on wine. But I was tired of having to drink what Laurence thought was the appropriate accompaniment to the evening's menu. It was not clear to me by what authority he took it upon himself to choose the wine for the table, especially when he was not treating us. And there was no danger of that.

'What about a chardonnay for a change?' I suggested. There was a silence. To date, Laurence's authority to order the wine had gone unchallenged.

'Dermot,' he began slowly, 'I wouldn't expect you to know this ...' his bottom lip curled until it reached the precise angle of contempt needed to unleash the response that was under preparation, 'Chablis *is* a chardonnay.' In the greater scheme of things it probably didn't matter that I did not know Chablis was a chardonnay, but I had to admit that, at that moment of the evening in King's Inns, I was humbled. Needless to say, Chablis arrived, so I moved on to the red.

Afric was a great fan of Ted's and decided to throw in the ball. 'He'll make a great judge but he'll be a big loss to the Library.'

Miriam agreed with Afric, which was no surprise because she usually does and anyway there isn't a woman in the place who isn't mad about Ted. 'Absolutely. He is the most accessible of colleagues, never too busy to help you.'

'As long as you are female,' Laurence chipped in in an unchivalrous reference to the fact that Ted's love of the lady barristers does not go unrequited. Laurence was particularly crusty this evening. Perhaps his Chablis was not up to scratch.

'Not fair, Laurence,' said Afric in support of Ted.

'Rubbish, Laurence,' added Miriam in support of Afric. 'It doesn't matter whether you are male or female, young or old. Every afternoon at four o'clock Ted has a queue of colleagues looking for advice.'

'And a gin and tonic,' Laurence added in an unnecessary reference to the fact that Ted is partial to refreshment after his day in court.

'Not fair either, Laurence,' said Afric.

'Not at all fair,' Miriam said. 'The way he works, he is entitled to his gin and tonic.'

'I don't know, Laurence, I'm inclined to agree with Afric and Miriam.' Mark decided that the conversation needed a new voice. 'I think he'll be a good judge. You can never be sure, of course. Until they're up there for a while, you never know what they'll be like. But, as far as Ted is concerned, there are no chips, no agendas, no scores to settle. I think he'll be alright. Do you not agree, Laurence, or are you just being awkward?'

Laurence was savouring his Chablis, perhaps trying to make up his mind finally as to whether or not it was up to scratch. I wasn't sure that he was ready for a major contribution to the debate. He was moving the grape around his mouth with considerable dexterity, indeed transparency. We awaited his opinion of the wine and of Ted. The performance culminated in a tapping together of his well-lubricated lips and an extravagant swallow. He gave judgment immediately, congratulating himself on the wine but more particularly on the fact that he had chosen it.

'A first class Chablis. I must say I have chosen well. Don't you agree? Particularly suitable for the evening that's in it,' Laurence pronounced. No one knew what attribute it was that made this wine particularly suitable for the evening that was in it, nor indeed what attribute of the evening Laurence had in mind.

Unfortunately, however, his satisfaction with the wine had done nothing for his opinion of Ted. 'Ted reminds me of Dermot,' he announced. I wondered what could be coming. 'I mean Dermot's chardonnay ... lightweight ... charming of course, but essentially lightweight. Ted has neither the intellectual depth nor the knowledge of the law that are required for the High Court. He would have been a perfect appointment to the Circuit Court.'

Laurence had not met Sonia before and was not to know that her father was a Circuit Court judge. Jimmy was unlikely to let this go. 'Hey. Hold on you pompous bollocks,' he said, in the vernacular. 'Have a bit more respect. Sonia's dad is the judge on the Western Circuit and, even if he wasn't, you're talking a load of rubbish. The Circuit Court is every bit as demanding as the High.'

It was Laurence's turn to feel the heat. He could not really be blamed. Sonia was only in the Library a few weeks and he had never met her before. 'I'm very sorry, Sonia,' he said graciously. 'I don't think I have had the pleasure of meeting you. I do apologise. Of course, my remarks were not in any way personal. I am a great admirer of your father.' It had to be said that Laurence rose to the occasion. He even had the decency to raise a blush, though that might have been the Chablis.

'That's all right. You weren't to know.' Sonia forgave charmingly and, if appearances were anything to go by, soared even higher in Jimmy's estimation.

It might have been a good idea to change the topic of conversation but, if it was, the idea did not occur to Laurence. 'Perhaps I might clarify?' Laurence prepared to dig deeper. 'I am a great fan of the Circuit Court and Circuit Court judges.'

'They'll all be thrilled about that,' Jimmy said.

'Indeed, in your dad's case, Sonia, he might well be a High Court judge yet,' Laurence continued, ignoring Jimmy.

'Actually, Laurence, he is quite happy on the Circuit Court bench. He loves his work and he loves the west and, by all accounts, he is not too bad at his job,' Sonia said, rejecting Laurence's generous offer of promotion for her father.

'Exactly what I was saying, Sonia. He's a splendid judge and would still be a splendid judge were he to go to the

High Court. But my point is that the High Court is more demanding than heretofore.' Laurence had no idea when to give up. 'Cases are more difficult, they're longer and there is more publicity. Ted just isn't up to it.' Laurence paused. I felt he hadn't finished, but Miriam came to a different conclusion and jumped in.

'You're wrong, Laurence. Ted is well up to the job. The most important quality for a judge is courtesy and he has that in spades. And as for intelligence, it would be unwise of you or anyone else to underestimate him,' she said.

'Hear hear,' Afric said.

'Perhaps, Miriam, but what about his experience, his practice?' Laurence wanted to know.

'What about it? He has a huge practice,' Miriam informed him.

'But where, Miriam? The Round Hall, that's where. Personal injury cases. "Did you blow your horn?" and lunch with the fellow from the insurance company. That's it.' At last it was out. It had been lurking, but now Laurence's real objection to Ted came to the surface.

Laurence spends his life in the Chancery Courts arguing about trusts and debentures and the like. Not a court the light of day reaches often. He has a high opinion of the intellectual worth and knowledge of the law of those practising alongside him, and believes that appointments to the High Court should be filled from this corner of the Bar.

'Laurence, that's a load of nonsense and you know it,' Afric was fired up and all the prettier for it. As she reached across the table, her breasts rested on her place in front of her. Laurence might have been distracted were he not at that moment engaged in a sip of his beloved wine. 'For my money the real advocates in this place are in the Round Hall,' Afric continued. 'Look at the names down the years: McCarthy, Walsh, Wood, FitzGerald. Are you telling me that they were chardonnays, not learned in the law? You fellas in 5 and 6 with your law reports and endless affidavits! That's the height of it. My money's on Ted.' Afric made her point with such spirit that her breasts were almost out of the little black number that she had brought in that morning, with the result that most of the red wine that I was pouring at the time ended up on the linen tablecloth.

Miriam came in behind Afric. 'She's right. You lot are far too full of yourselves, far too pedantic and far too dull.' It didn't seem to matter to Miriam that Afric had said none of those things. 'And what's more, you're too long-winded also.' Pleased with herself, she took another sip of wine.

Laurence, riding one of his favourite horses, was in his element. The fact that he was riding alone did not deter him. For Laurence, real lawyers devote their lives to fee farm grants and the 'rule against perpetuities'. There is nothing prurient about 'lifting the veil' and 'protection of minorities' has nothing to do with ethnic groupings. As far as Laurence and his like are concerned, Round Hall lawyers bring the Bar into disrepute with their arms full of briefs and quick settlements.

Mark realised that this conversation was going nowhere. It was an argument that had been aired forever at least and was not going to be resolved in the course of Ted's benching. 'Alright,' he intervened, 'enough is enough. It's Friday and maybe we can find a less contentious topic of conversation. Perhaps we might at least agree that Ted deserves his appointment to the Bench, and let time decide whether or not the jurisdiction will suit him?'

'Here's to Ted.' Afric raised her glass. Laurence followed suit. One by one our glasses were raised and clinked and emptied, making it necessary for Laurence to call again on the grapevine.

Dinner was coming to an end. Mr Kilkelly was going from table to table offering snuff. Laurence encouraged us to agree on a verdict on the meal for recording in the Dining Book. After discussion, 'suitable' was the word decided on. Laurence's choice again. Everyone signed an early edition of *The Military Life of Hannibal, Vol. I*, with which the guest of honour was to be presented. The only thing to recommend it was that Ted wouldn't have already read it. As these final rituals took place, the former chief justices, frowning from their frames on the walls of the dining hall, seemed to mellow momentarily, signalling their approval of how the evening had gone.

Mr Kilkelly waited for silence. When it arrived, he filled it with the words *'Benedicto benedicatur'*. This was the cue for the presiding bencher to lead Ted to the top of the aisle where he could retrace his steps into oblivion. Just before he commenced this journey, the most junior barrister present stepped forward and, apologising for the subject matter of the book, she made the presentation. Ted replied with an extravagant kiss on both cheeks and the applause commenced.

The return journey was not as intimidating. For one thing there had been no shortage of wine at the benchers' table and also a certain amount of adaptation had already taken place. The benchers bowed their way to their room upstairs and we retreated to our Bar-room where we had a coffee before making our way to the après-benching in the Distillery.

Whether you are coming or going, the short distance between the Distillery, an extension of the Law Library, and King's Inns is the same. However, somehow the journey back seems longer and so, while there was no shortage of drink in the Inns, and there would be no shortage in the Distillery, it seemed prudent to stop off briefly in The Tap.

There was a friendly atmosphere in the pub where the locals were enjoying their end-of-week pints. A football match was on the telly in one corner and a game of darts was underway in another. Neither the patrons nor The Tap's accountants needed the endorsement of these members of the Honorable Society. However, in they arrived in their hordes. Crème-de-menthe frappés for the ladies in black and pints for the lads in their three-piece suits, some of whom were still wearing their gowns from dinner. Not one for pints, Laurence was discussing the wine list with the barman. It was time to go when Laurence informed him that there was nothing on it that he could drink. The hordes moved on and The Tap returned to its erstwhile harmony.

I had never been at a benching that was so well attended. In the Distillery, members of the Bar and Bench mingled as freely as the wine flowed. An outsider could not have been blamed for concluding that this was a homogeneous gathering of fun-loving lawyers – Bar and Bench at play. No sign of the tension that might be expected to exist between them, no sign of the wounds inflicted by one on the other in court in recent days. Among the Bar itself, no sign of competition or jealousy. An uncomplicated coming together of judges and barristers to celebrate a new arrival.

This was an ideal opportunity for the Ronald Brownings of this world. They were there to ingratiate themselves with those members of the Bench who were willing to encourage them. I could see Ronald working the room. No judge or senior barrister was left out. Just the right word in the right ear. A mention of golf here, a recent decision there, how well such-and-such cross-examination had gone, and so on. No danger whatever of Ronald being here after eleven. No danger whatever of Ronald dropping his guard, which couldn't be said of many of his colleagues, who would be getting taxis home in the early hours.

One of the advantages of this venue is its atrium that allows you the freedom to come and go, to enter and exit circles and conversations with ease. You can move away a little from the crowd should you choose to do so.

At the far end of the atrium is a goldfish pond and Hugh Scott, S.C. took himself off to its low wall for a smoke and gentle flirtation. Hugh is a lovely shy fellow who would not be able to chat up a pretty Junior unless he has more alcohol than is advisable. On this occasion, the Junior seemed enthralled by what was likely to be a not-very-entertaining account of a not-very-entertaining case. However, her body language suggested that the pursuit was not without hope.

They were both sitting on the low wall, not a goldfish in sight. It could have been a garden scene in summer were it not for the fact that it was November and they were indoors. Hugh, his hands wrapped around his knees, appeared to be fully in control as he rocked gently forwards and backwards, drawing elegantly on his cigarette from time to time. The receptive Junior was hanging on every rock. Unfortunately, Hugh was not as fully in control as he thought and one of his rocks tilted his balance in favour of the goldfish. The not-very-loyal Junior promptly disappeared, leaving it to others to fish her Silk out of the water.

I thought that Laurence might have had enough of everyone in the Inns. On the contrary, displaying the tenacity of people like him, there he was, a glass of Chablis in one hand and a glass of claret in the other, hanging on every word of Mr Justice Madden, long-serving member of the Supreme Court. I couldn't help overhearing.

'What do you think of our recent appointments, Judge?' Laurence asked. Madden's eyes lit up. This was a favourite topic. 'In my opinion there is not enough intellectual weight coming into the Superior Courts,' he continued. I knew from earlier that Laurence would have liked to go on but Madden wasn't letting him.

'I couldn't agree with you more, Laurence. Indeed, it is quite a coincidence that you ask me because some of us were just saying the same thing over dinner.'

'As you say, Judge, quite a coincidence.' Laurence was sipping his red and white alternately.

'Of course, we weren't thinking of Ted,' Madden made clear.

'Of course not, Judge.' Lawrence understood perfectly.

'A splendid appointment. The essence of courtesy and politeness. And if he hasn't had much experience in the Chancery Courts, I have no doubt that he will pick it up quickly. Smart chap, Ted.'

'I am in complete agreement, Judge. I was saying the same thing over dinner.'

'But, leaving Ted aside,' Madden continued, 'your point is a good one. For example, take many of our recent appointments. Could you in honesty say that they are up to the heavier cases? It seems to me that it's more about political connection than excellence as an advocate. What do you think, Laurence?' No doubt Laurence would have loved to tell him what he thought, but Madden resumed before he had a chance. 'Success at the Bar seems to play second fiddle to arranging golf classics,' Madden said.

Laurence saw his chance. 'Take your own elevation, Judge,' a consideration certain to gain Madden's full attention. 'When you were appointed, you had one of the biggest practices at the Bar.'

'Nice of you to say so, Laurence. The biggest probably,' Madden added.

'Absolutely. And not just that. There was no court that you did not appear in.'

The judge seemed very impressed with Laurence. 'Exactly. In my time at the bar, we did everything.'

'For heaven's sake, Judge, some of our recent appointments spent more time in Leinster House than in the Four Courts.' Laurence sipped away.

'It's all changed, Laurence. All changed.' Madden seemed to have forgotten the countless speeches he had written at election time, not to mention his occupation of Government Buildings as soon as a judicial vacancy was announced.

There wasn't another pair on the planet that evening as *ad idem* as Laurence and Mr Justice Madden. Madden's eyes were beginning to mist over as he recalled a bygone era when damsels danced at crossroads and judges were appointed on merit.

I couldn't listen to any more and so went in search of Afric. It didn't take long. There she was, as ever, surrounded by a bevy of Silks and judges. Meanwhile, the bar staff were doing the rounds with every conceivable concoction of alcohol, ensuring that Ted's hospitality was fully and freely availed of. I treated myself to an advocaat and brandy. Having spotted Afric, the next person to come into my view, not surprisingly, was Mr Justice Fleming.

Fleming's demeanour suggested that he had managed to put the complexities of the case at hearing before him out of his mind, which was precisely where he was himself at that moment. In a word, he had unwound. Evidence for this observation was the presence of his large hand on Afric's left buttock. It was odds on at this point in the evening that his hand would be on someone's. Afric was doing her utmost, consistent with discretion, to free herself and her buttock from Fleming's attention, but without success. At this stage in his career, Fleming had considerable experience and it wasn't easy for a target to disengage without causing a scene.

Fleming chose wisely. There are many female barristers who wouldn't bat an eyelid at pointing out to him where precisely his hand may or may not go. Afric is not one of these. Psychoanalysts would have a field day analysing why this is so. Whatever their conclusion, there remains the fact that it is just not her way. And so she stood there, waiting to be rescued.

By now I was pretty well unwound myself, and was managing to keep at bay thoughts of an early night and a weekend assault on my paperwork. A feeling of holistic well-being, that I was unlikely to shake off, had overtaken me. As I kept reminding myself, things were going well. We were moving on to a nightclub and I hoped Afric would join us. She was so pleased to be rescued from Fleming that she couldn't refuse. As we crossed the Halpenny Bridge on our way to Leeson Street, a full moon illuminated the dome of the Four Courts and the Liffey beneath.

It must have been about two. The dance-floor was packed with Friday night revellers. Afric and I managed to find ourselves a less crowded corner with a comfortable sofa, a table for our bottle of wine and a slice of the dance-floor in case the mood took us. I didn't want anything else. I was happy with what we had – the music, the soft light – away from the wandering hands of Fleming. I didn't know where the night might lead and I thought better of anticipating it in too much detail.

We were dancing. Neither of us had said anything for a while, Afric for longer. I was beginning to wonder if she had fallen asleep. She was leaning Tower-of-Pisa-like against me. She had her arms around my waist and my nose was buried in her neck. This was as close to heaven as it got.

All of a sudden, I felt a prodding on my chest. She was up on her tiptoes and whispering in my ear.

'Dermot, I don't feel so well.'

'How not so well?'

'No time to lose,' she replied.

We were across the dance-floor and out of the nightclub in a moment, once again looking for a quiet, dark corner where we could mind our own business. We barely made it. Poor Afric. The moon was not seeing her at her most elegant that evening in the car park at the back of the nightclub.

If life is what happens when you are making plans, this wasn't a bad illustration. I hailed a taxi and delivered Afric to her apartment off the South Circular Road. It wasn't really the night to be invited in for coffee.

'I'm sorry, Dermot,' she mimed, giving me a kiss on the cheek and, pale as a sheet, departing.

I raced the dawn to Seapoint, closing the door just in time.

DOWN FROM DUBLIN

Devils, like their masters, come in all shapes and sizes. Some even become like their masters. There are portly devils, short devils, thin and tall devils. Some are extraordinarily bright, others extraordinarily less so. Some hardly stop talking. For others, words are like an endangered species. One is shy and slips through the door of the Law Library sideways, another strides through like a colossus. And that's just the male of the species.

In the beginning, female devils were few and far between. The Law Library was something of a male preserve, a colonial club. But no longer. Like their male counterparts, female devils too come in all shapes and sizes. Unfortunately.

According to the Oxford Dictionary, a devil is 'the chief spirit of evil and enemy of God ... often depicted as a human figure with horns, cloven hooves and tail'. Harsh, but close enough. In Malaysia, a devil is a ghost and many a master would agree with this, especially when he is looking for his devil at around half nine on a Monday morning.

It used to be that the devil paid his master a fee for the privilege of devilling with him. As a *quid pro quo*, the devil felt entitled to dip into his master's practice, thereby ensuring that winds would not blow too chill when the devilling year ended. In more recent times, the convention of paying the master a fee has been dropped unilaterally, although the entitlement to dip into the master's practice has survived. The postmodern thinking, at least on one side of the equation, is that the person providing the service should also pay for it and, accordingly, the master should pay the devil for the privilege of teaching him.

Norman is constructed a bit like a snowman. A pair of outsized spectacles rest on his wine-soaked nose. He is about ten years older than me, indeed about ten years older than everyone. He comes from another life, the identity of which has never been disclosed. There are two notable things about Norman: he is not the brightest and he is utterly oblivious to the fact. While, in the fullness of time, these characteristics would become clear to me, I wasn't sufficiently perceptive to pick them up in the course of our first meeting a year earlier. This was a perfunctory sort of appointment at which I sought no more than to confirm that Norman existed and had been called to the Bar. All he wanted to be sure of was that I was actually in practice. I did notice that he dressed impeccably and that he polished his shoes. What more could one want in a devil? Certainly, there was nothing in the course of this encounter to suggest that this life-long relationship should not go ahead.

Its going ahead commenced on the first day of the Hilary Term, that is to say a term late, for traditionally devils embark on their devilling year on the first day of the Michaelmas Term, which is the first Monday in October. For reasons that had to do with 'tidying up some loose ends' from his previous unidentified existence, Norman chose to defer his debut until after Christmas. This exception apart, he is punctual to a fault. Indeed, he is most things to a fault.

As my first case of the New Year was bringing me out on circuit, I thought this would be a good opportunity for some quality time with my new devil. After all, we had ground to make up.

Of course, bonding between master and devil requires privacy and I had not banked on a phone call from Mr Phillips on the last day of the Christmas vacation telling me to collect him at his office in Fitzwilliam Square at eight thirty the following morning. I was grateful to Mr Phillips for enabling me to start the new term with a new brief from his office. But he might have asked me for a lift rather than telling me that he was taking one. And he might have met me at the Four Courts, where I was collecting Norman, or somewhere in between. It was only a gesture I was looking for.

Anyway, these were minor irritations and so, at half past eight, I arrived outside the office of Walsh & Phillips, my newly acquired devil in tow. There was no sign of Phillips. I sent Norman in to announce our arrival while I held on to the double yellow lines outside.

Norman seemed to be gone forever, and when he did reappear it was to say that Phillips would join us shortly. Not shortly enough for Garda Fitzgibbon from Store Street Station, who wasn't impressed by my plea that I was collecting my solicitor en route to the citadel of justice in Wicklow. Muttering that I should know better, he fined me and went on his way.

As soon as Phillips got into the car, I told him about Garda Fitzgibbon and the fine, but he seemed to miss the point. He was sure I was aware of their excellent parking facilities at the rear of their building. Obviously, he had an inflated notion of the volume of work I was doing for his office.

By way of explanation for the fact that he had kept us waiting for half an hour, he told us that it was not at all convenient to have to spend the day in Wicklow. Time out of his office was money, he moaned. His eternal apprentices, Amy and Sophie, were on a mental health day so they could not stand in for him. Anyway, the client was keen that he should attend in person, and so here he was.

Somewhere between the jigs and the reels, it had been necessary for Phillips to do some urgent dictation before joining Norman and I in the car. He had given a tape to his secretary as he was leaving but that wasn't the end of it. There was more to be done and, if I didn't mind turning off the radio, with a bit of luck and the wind behind us, he might get another tape done between here and Wicklow.

In silence, apart from the drone of dictation, we travelled our route to Wicklow. Through the furry Glen of the Downs we drove, deeper and deeper into the Garden of Ireland: past Fly Fishers, the emporium that dresses barristers for weekends and others for grouse shooting in Balmoral; through Ashford, where you might stop to buy a cone if it's sunny and you're on your way to Brittas Bay; then Mount Usher where you might go in May for the rhododendrons; and, finally, as Phillips reached the end of the tape, arriving in the town that is home to the jurisprudence of the county.

Judge Hunter is tall, thin and of ascetic appearance. With his sparse silver hair he resembles an elderly Jesuit. He loves his Circuit, which has its headquarters in Wicklow, and tends it from Tuesday to Friday each week of the law term. On the remaining three days he lives by himself in a large country house on a few acres outside the town.

He has not always been a recluse. Rumour has it that when he was a young barrister he fell madly in love with a beautiful solicitor from Rathdrum. Nothing seemed surer than, as soon as his practice took off, they would make their way down the aisle. But fate intervened and struck down the diva from Rathdrum through a skiing accident in the Pyrenees.

The young barrister never recovered. He threw himself into his practice and, in the fullness of time, was appointed a Circuit Court judge. He reads extensively and has an enviable music collection. His only friend is the parish priest who visits him every Sunday evening, when they enjoy a whiskey together and a game of chess.

The court sits at ten thirty every morning. Judge Hunter would probably have no problem starting earlier. After all, he is up from dawn. However, the solicitors and the barristers practising in his court persuaded him not to start earlier as they needed that time for their consultations and negotiations. He gets the better of them at the other end of the day, for there is no such thing as the court rising at four o'clock. 'Justice delayed is justice denied' is one of his most repeated maxims. He is determined that there will be no backlog of litigation on his Circuit. Folklore has it that one year he gave his last judgment at midnight on Christmas Eve.

Phillips had no intention of being in Wicklow until Christmas Eve, nor indeed until midnight. If he could at all, he would be out by lunch hour. After all, if Wicklow was Judge Hunter's kingdom, Fitzwilliam Square was his and the sooner he got back there the better.

Finding my way to the courthouse in Wicklow was the easy part. I had been told that there were two courtrooms but I did not know the whereabouts of either of them. More importantly, I did not know where the Bar-room was. For reasons presumably known to someone, it was not thought necessary to erect a signpost within the building or to put names on the doors. Consequently, the visiting barrister has to poke his head into a number of irrelevant rooms before arriving at his destination.

Happily, I was spared this embarrassment as Norman had been in the courthouse before and was familiar with the territory, or so he thought. Confidently, he led me on a tour of the building, up, down, in and out. We went from the basement full of dusty documents up to the attic, which was like an antique shop with its collection of typewriters, furniture and even an old bicycle. We looked into rooms that appeared as if they hadn't been occupied for a hundred years, finally, by this labyrinthine route, finding the Bar-room.

The Bar-room is a sanctuary for solicitors and barristers alike, a retreat from clients and their endless exhortations. Within, barristers robe for court, discuss their cases with their solicitors, and initiate negotiations with their opposite numbers. Without, the principals await.

By and large, these rooms are dreary places, dark and dank. The one in Wicklow was no exception. An oval-shaped mahogany table dominated the room. There were not enough chairs to go around and I happened to select the one reserved for the recently retired president of the Wicklow Solicitors Association who, I was assured, would be along any moment. There was no window to allow in the winter light. From three of the four walls the elderly Jesuit's predecessors kept an eye on the proceedings. The elderly Jesuit himself hung above the fireplace. The table was full of wigs and gowns, briefs and brollies, papers and reports. The gloom was redeemed only by the glow from the fire that the county registrar lit when the court was sitting ... and of course, the welcome.

Derek Delahunt, the leader of the Circuit, greeted me warmly. Derek is a substantial barrister with a substantial practice. Just as the oval table dominated the room, Derek dominates the Circuit. He likes nothing better than an audience and, most evenings after court, he is to be found in the Wicklow Arms Hotel surrounded by young and old of the Circuit.

Derek is in his mid-fifties. Some years earlier, he toyed with the idea of taking silk. Once he thought about it, he realised how much he likes his lot in Wicklow. He likes the small pond, his colleagues, and the solicitors for whom he works. He works hard. Indeed he is a workaholic and an insomniac, a useful combination for a barrister. He manages on five hours' sleep, which he begins routinely at midnight so that, from shortly after five in the morning, he is at his desk turning over his paperwork and keeping his solicitors happy. Taking silk would have meant many changes. One of these, a daily return trip to Dublin, didn't appeal to him. Derek opted for continuity and remains a Junior in Wicklow. He likes it when colleagues travel from Dublin and always gives them a warm welcome.

'To what do we owe this pleasure?' Derek asked.

'An allegedly defective car and a discerning solicitor in Fitzwilliam Square, Derek,' I replied.

'Sure it wouldn't be you, Mac, if it wasn't a posh case.'

'Would that it were so, Derek.'

'A defective car you say. It wouldn't be O'Connor *v.* Wicklow Garages, would it?'

'The very case. I suppose you're in it.'

'I'm for the plaintiff, Mac. The principal of our local school. I don't think even you and your posh friend from Fitzwilliam Square could defend this one.'

'I don't know about that. As far as we are concerned, we have a full defence.'

'I'm sure you have. I've never known a solicitor from Fitzwilliam Square not to have a full defence. What is it this time?'

'To cut a long story short, we shouldn't be here at all.'

'But your client sold us the car,' Derek said, baffled.

'No, that's the point. Wicklow Garages sold the car.'

'But they're in liquidation.'

'I know that. That's your problem, not ours.'

'But your client supplied the car to them.'

'No, they didn't. I act for Asemota (Ireland) Ltd. Your car was supplied to Wicklow Garages by Asemota (UK) Ltd.'

'Hold on now, Mac, hold on. Have I got this right? You've come all the way from Dublin for this case, with your fancy solicitor from Fitzwilliam Square, and your defence is that your client Asemota (Ireland) Ltd is not liable. Asemota (UK) Ltd, who is not your client, is liable. Is that it?'

'In a nutshell.'

Derek didn't seem too impressed by corporate structures. Phillips and Norman joined us.

'Dermot, where are we in the list?' Phillips had no problem interrupting my discussion with Derek. 'I assume that as we're down from Dublin we'll be taken first.' He was clearly out of touch with how things were done on Circuit nowadays.

'Well down, unfortunately.'

'What are you going to do? I have some very important meetings this afternoon. I have to be away by lunch hour.'

'There's nothing I can do,' I replied.

'Nothing?'

'Absolutely nothing. We are where we are,' I added profoundly.

'You could always make a special application,' Derek was addressing Phillips, 'as you're down from Dublin.'

I began to robe for court. As I did so, I was chatting with colleagues and completely forgot about my new devil. Suddenly I caught sight of him. There he stood in the middle of the busy Bar-room, naked from the waist up. Oblivious to the attention he was receiving from the solicitors and barristers around him, Norman was changing his shirt. Not for him the corner of the room or the en suite. No, Norman chose the centre of the floor, where flames from the fire bounced off his bare chest.

Phillips whisked me off to the only consultation room in the entire building, which somehow he had managed to commandeer. In case he might not find the room in which he had earlier deposited Mr Asemota, he had placed a sign bearing the name 'Walsh & Phillips' on the door. I could only assume that he had brought it down with him from Dublin as it was unlikely to be available in Wicklow. Reserving the only consultation room was not likely to endear him to the local solicitors. But then that may not have been his priority, such was the urgency of his business back in town.

'Mr Asemota, I would like you to meet your counsel, Dermot McNamara,' Phillips said, as soon as we entered the occupied territory. 'Dermot specialises in contract law and practises on the Circuit here as well as in Dublin.'

I knew enough about contract law to know that there was an element of misrepresentation in Phillips's introduction. However, I wasn't going to contradict him.

'Very pleased to meet you, Mr McNamara,' our client said courteously. Mr Asemota was everything you would expect of a gentleman from the land of the rising sun. He was small in stature and thin, with impeccably groomed dark hair. His manner was polite and not assertive. He set out for me the facts of our case precisely and clearly, and such was his presentation and my attention that, for the second time since we arrived in Wicklow, I had completely forgotten about Norman.

The door burst open. My devil burst in.

'He wasn't very helpful, Dermot,' Norman announced. I was in the dark and so were Phillips and Asemota.

'Who wasn't very helpful, Norman?' I asked, seeking light.

'The judge.'

'Wasn't helpful to whom?'

'To Mr Phillips. '

'What do you mean the judge wasn't very helpful to Mr Phillips?'

'Precisely that. I went to the judge in his room ...'

'In his chambers, Norman,' I corrected.

'In his chambers, and asked him could he take our case first.'

'You did *what?*'

'I asked Judge Hunter if he could take our case first.'

'Norman, please tell me you're not serious.'

'But I am, Dermot.'

'And what did he say?'

'He asked me who I was and how long I was at the Bar.'

'And what did you tell him?'

'I told him it was my first day.'

'And did he ask you anything else?'

'He asked me who I was devilling with.'

'And did you tell him?'

'I did,' Norman said proudly.

'And did Judge Hunter say anything else?'

'He said he wanted to see you at the call-over of the list.'

I looked at my watch. Half past ten. As if electrocuted, I shot to my feet, just about managing to gather my wig and my papers, and was gone.

'Is Mr McNamara in court?' I heard the registrar enquire as I entered the courtroom, which was packed for the first day of sessions.

'Here, My Lord,' I barely heard myself announce as I did my best to make my way through the throng of barristers, solicitors, litigants, witnesses and some members of the Wicklow public with nothing better to do. 'I'm terribly sorry, My Lord. I have only just heard.' By now I was at the front of the court, utterly alone.

'Mr McNamara.'

This was my first appearance before Judge Hunter. By reputation, he was courteous and understanding of human failing. For a predicament such as mine at that moment, there were worse draws. Lynx-eyed, he sat above me, watching the arrival of his prey. He was too thin, I thought, as I saw him for the first time.

'Yes, My Lord.' I could sense the ripple of anticipation running around the courtroom like a Mexican wave.

'I had a visitor, Mr McNamara …' he said and then paused, the packed court in the palm of his hands, 'a few minutes ago.'

'Yes, My Lord.'

'He said his name was Nelson. Norman Nelson he said his name was.'

'Yes, My Lord.'

'He said he was a barrister, Mr McNamara. It was his first day in practice.'

'Yes, My Lord.'

'Apparently he should have started in October with everyone else, but that wasn't possible and so he is starting today.'

'Yes, My Lord.'

'And that he is devilling with you, Mr McNamara.'

'That is correct, My Lord.'

'Do you know what he wanted, Mr McNamara?' I had a feeling that this was what is known as a rhetorical question, but I thought it might be rude not to reply.

'Yes, My Lord.'

'He wanted to know if I would give your case priority,' Hunter said, ignoring my reply. One of the advantages of being a judge is that you can be a law unto yourself. 'And,

Mr McNamara, when I asked him why he wanted priority, do you know what his reply was?'

This time I knew a rhetorical question when I saw one and so said nothing.

'Well, Mr McNamara, do you?' Wrong again.

'I have an idea, My Lord, but that was not ...'

'Well, I'll tell you, Mr McNamara.' The judge seemed a bit confused about rhetorical questions himself. But no one in court was complaining. Hunter was in full judicial flight. Those present hung on every syllable, every gesticulation. 'He told me that you are instructed by a top solicitor in Dublin who has to be back in his office in Fitzwilliam Square as soon as possible for some important meetings. Apparently, he doesn't have all day to hang around Wicklow.'

More than I hoped Norman was present to witness the mess he had got me into, I hoped that Phillips had stayed in the consultation room with the client. While the Bar of Wicklow enjoyed this early entertainment, I tried to think of something to say. Unfortunately.

'That is correct, My Lord.'

'What is correct, Mr McNamara? That your solicitor doesn't have all day to hang around Wicklow?'

'No, My Lord.'

'Well, what then?'

'That my solicitor is a leading solicitor in Dublin.'

'And does that entitle him to priority when he comes to Wicklow?'

'Not at all, My Lord. On the contrary ...'

'Mr McNamara, your devil sought priority for your case.'

'I know, My Lord. It's all been a frightful mistake. I am terribly sorry.' I was hoping that that might be the end of the matter. Just at that moment, I felt my gown being tugged. It was Phillips, a little breathless.

118

'Did you ask him?' he wanted to know. 'Did you ask him for priority?' Unfortunately, Phillips did not speak as quietly as he might have.

'Is this your leading solicitor from Dublin, Mr McNamara?'

'It is. Mr Phillips, My Lord,' I said, introducing my solicitor.

'I gather, Mr Phillips, that you are anxious to get back to Dublin?'

Phillips was not the sort of person who needed much by way of an invitation. 'I am, My Lord. I have a number of important matters to attend to this afternoon. I would be extremely grateful if you could hear my case first.' Priority was not enough apparently. Phillips wanted his case heard first.

'Mr Phillips, you are not suggesting, or are you, that your important matters in Dublin are more important than those of your colleagues here in Wicklow?'

'Oh no, My Lord. I am not suggesting any such thing. I am sure the solicitors here are very busy also. However, if there is some way Your Lordship could ...'

'By any chance is your client elderly or incapacitated in any way?'

'Oh no, My Lord, he's from Japan.'

'From Japan, Mr Phillips? That doesn't entitle him to priority, surely?'

'No, it doesn't, My Lord. All I am saying is that he is neither elderly nor incapacitated. Merely that he is from Japan. He doesn't need priority. I do.'

'Have you anything to add, Mr McNamara?' Hunter had tired of Phillips and turned to me.

'No, My Lord. I am terribly sorry. A dreadful mistake. I will be having a word with Mr Nelson.'

'Who is against you, Mr McNamara?'

'I am, My Lord,' Derek replied.

'Thank you, Mr Delahunt. Do you see any reason why Mr McNamara's case should be given priority?'

'In the ordinary way, I would have no difficulty facilitating my friend.' In Derek's case, this was probably true. 'However, I have to point out that the plaintiff in this case is the principal of our local school and it would be very inconvenient for him, not to mention his students, if his case were to come on before four o'clock.'

'That settles it then, gentlemen. There is nothing further to be said. Not before four o'clock. Now, we have a long list to get through so maybe we could get on to the real business of the day.'

As I drove Phillips to the train that would stop briefly in Wicklow, he assured me that he would be back for 'not before four o'clock'.

'It might be wiser to stay,' I suggested.

'But why?'

'Well, it's just that when it comes to court, little is certain,' I tried to explain.

'But didn't the judge himself say "not before four o'clock"?' Phillips said. 'And isn't he the boss?' I agreed that indeed he was. 'So why on earth would I spend the next five hours hanging around Wicklow?' reasoned Philips. Why on earth indeed. There seemed little point in listing the town's attractions. They would not be enough to detain a busy solicitor like Mr Phillips.

'How do you make money hanging around a godforsaken place like this?' Phillips wanted to know as he boarded the train that would take him to his corporate client who, at that moment, was landing from America.

Mr Asemota too was anxious to move on. Very politely, he asked to be excused. There were cars out there to be sold and, if I didn't mind, he too would be back 'not before four o'clock'. I had no jurisdiction over Phillips but, in his

120

absence, I felt that I had some authority as far as Mr Asemota was concerned. I suggested that he might put his head in at around two to see how the list was going.

The day had hardly begun and I was on my own, except for Norman of course, whom I had placed in the well of the court under strict instructions to look and listen but, under no circumstances, to speak.

At lunchtime, Derek kindly invited my devil and I to cross the road for a sandwich and the inevitable vegetable soup. From the chat over lunch, it was clear that we were in for the long haul. Despite the judge's best efforts, the list was not budging and if the right-of-way case, which was next up, got going we could throw our hat at it for the day. It seemed I could now let go of the fear that my case might suddenly be called on with neither solicitor nor client present.

At half past two I was back in the Bar-room insisting on my share of the fire. Outside, the day was darkening and it was becoming colder by the minute. Snow was a risk and a night in Wicklow couldn't be ruled out. After the frenzy that fills every courthouse in the land at around half past ten in the morning, especially on the first day of sessions, the pace had settled somewhat. The urgency attached to each case when the list was called diminished as the day dragged on and the realisation dawned that the case might not be reached until later in the week, if at all.

At about twenty-five to three, my devil burst in for the second time that day. 'We're on!' he roared across the fire.

'But it's not four o'clock,' I pointed out. The clock above the door confirmed this even without taking into account its inclination to run ten minutes fast.

'The case has just been called and the judge is looking for you.' Once again, I grabbed everything in sight and headed faster than I could for the courtroom.

'I am sorry, My Lord.' I seemed to be doing a lot of apologising to Judge Hunter today. 'I gather Your Lordship is looking for me.'

'I am not looking for you as such, Mr McNamara. But the case of O'Connor *v.* Wicklow Garages Ltd and Asemota (Ireland) Ltd has just been called by the registrar and, if my memory serves me, you are for one of the parties. Is that not correct?'

'It is, My Lord.'

'I am ready to hear it.'

'But I understood there was a right-of-way case ... twenty witnesses ... that would take the rest of the day?'

'There was and there is. But common sense has prevailed. Settlement talks are taking place and the parties have requested a short adjournment. The case may not go on.'

What was I to do? Phillips wasn't due for over an hour. I had no idea where Asemota was. 'Your Lordship did say "not before four o'clock".'

'And you, Mr McNamara, were looking for priority. Or at least your devil was. And your solicitor was keen to get back to Dublin.' His Lordship knew how to handle his point. I sensed the amusement of those present.

'I fully understand what you are saying, but unfortunately ...'

I wasn't allowed to continue. Judge Hunter didn't have to explain but he did anyway. 'Mr Delahunt tells me that his client's situation has changed. Instead of not being able to be here before four o'clock on account of his duties at our local school, he now finds that he can't be here after four o'clock as his senior team has an important match at four thirty.'

There was nothing else for it. The bullet had to be bitten. 'My Lord.'

'Yes, Mr McNamara.'

'I have a difficulty.'

'And what is that?'

'When Your Lordship said "not before four o'clock" I took Your Lordship at your word ...'

'Yes, Mr McNamara?' The judge's tone was just a little menacing. I wasn't getting this right.

'What I mean is, I assumed when you said "not before four o'clock", that you meant not before four o'clock.' The logic of my assumption was unassailable, but I didn't feel I was getting it across.

'Precisely what I meant, Mr McNamara. Unless of course the circumstances changed, in which event your case would be heard before four o'clock.'

'Unfortunately I misunderstood Your Lordship so that, when Mr Phillips asked me if it would be alright if he returned to Dublin – a very important client flying in from New York – I told him it would, as long as he was back by four.'

'That is too late for the plaintiff, Mr McNamara.'

'I know that now, My Lord.'

'And what about your client? Is he here?'

'My client is from Japan, My Lord.'

'I know that but is he here, Mr McNamara?'

'He's not, My Lord.'

'I suppose you told him he could go back to Japan?' Those in court found the judge's humour hilarious.

'No, My Lord.' I felt my gown being tugged furiously. I looked around. Norman was pointing to the back of the courtroom where Asemota, with his hands joined, was rocking forwards and backwards, indicating his presence. 'My client is here after all, My Lord.'

'Well, in that event, perhaps we can proceed with the case, Mr McNamara, and let the plaintiff away to his important duties?'

'Without Mr Phillips, My Lord?'

Derek rose to his feet. 'Yes, Mr Delahunt?' said Hunter.

'It might be of assistance if I tell Your Lordship that my client will agree to an adjournment of his case if that would assist Mr McNamara.'

'That's very generous of your client, Mr Delahunt. Well, Mr McNamara?'

How would I tell Phillips that his case was adjourned?

Hunter seemed to read my mind. 'Well then the case goes on,' he said.

How would I tell Phillips that his case had been heard?

'Really, Mr McNamara, it's one or the other.' Hunter's patience was exhausted. 'Either the case goes on or is adjourned. The plaintiff is most obliging and, as Mr Delahunt has explained, cannot be here after four o'clock.'

I simply had to elect. 'I understand, My Lord. In that event ... the case must ... go on,' I heard my voice say.

'Very wise, Mr McNamara, if I may say so,' Hunter said encouragingly.

'I hope so, My Lord,' I said quietly.

At precisely fifteen minutes to three by the clock above the bench, Aindreas O'Connor, the principal of the local secondary school, took the Bible in his right hand and swore to tell the entire truth. Derek took him through his evidence. He could have done it in his sleep.

A year earlier, Mr O'Connor had walked into the showrooms of Wicklow Garages on the edge of the town in search of a car. An hour later he drove out in a spanking new Asemota. He collected his wife and they went for a spin around the Garden of Ireland. It was the only journey in his new car that he would enjoy.

Next day, the problems began. They were small at first: the sunroof, electric windows, heating. Then the problems escalated. When he turned on the ignition there was a noise over and above the noise of the engine. The steering pulled to the left so that, if he took his hands off the steering wheel for a moment, he very quickly found himself and his car up on the footpath.

In the beginning, the garage was very helpful. Each time Mr O'Connor drove in with a complaint, he was listened to and the car was taken off him and returned the following day. But Mr O'Connor was becoming increasingly unhappy with his visits and the garage increasingly unhappy with him. The final straw was when the brakes failed as he approached a just-turned-red traffic light. He sailed through, a serious collision only avoided by the alertness of the other driver.

The principal of the local school had had enough. Wicklow Garages could have their car back and he would have his money. Unfortunately, commerce in Wicklow was not as simple as that. Wicklow Garages would take back the car all right but only to send it to England to see what the manufacturer had to say. Returning Mr O'Connor's money was not an option. He went to his solicitor and proceedings began.

Mr O'Connor's solicitor liked to keep counsel's involvement in a case to a minimum. He attended to the preliminary paperwork himself and took responsibility for the early decisions such as who to sue. In this instance, Wicklow Garages Ltd was the primary defendant. His solicitor called on his considerable experience and threw in Asemota (Ireland) Ltd for good measure. It was likely that Asemota (Ireland) Ltd had supplied the car to Wicklow Garages in the first place. This proved just as well because, no sooner had the proceedings been instituted, when Wicklow Garages, perhaps not surprisingly, went into liquidation.

By the time Derek sat down, having completed his examination of the plaintiff, any neutral observer would have been forgiven for thinking that the case was an open and shut affair. Mr O'Connor's purchase had clearly turned out to be seriously defective and, if Wicklow Garages couldn't cough up due to their demise, Asemota (Ireland) Ltd, the party that supplied the car to the garage, would have to accept responsibility. It was as clear as daylight.

The plaintiff, assuming that his evidential contribution to the proceedings was over once his counsel sat down, was off to the football match.

'Do stay in the witness box, Mr O'Connor,' Judge Hunter urged. 'Mr McNamara may want to ask you a few questions.' Hunter seemed to emphasise the word 'few'.

'Thank you, My Lord. Mr O'Connor, you bought your car from Wicklow Garages, isn't that so?' I began.

'It is, Mr McNamara.'

'And that garage has gone into liquidation, isn't that so?'

'It is.'

'And therefore a judgment against the garage is of no use to you, isn't that so?'

'It is.'

'So, you seek a judgment against my client, Asemota (Ireland) Ltd, isn't that right?'

'Yes.'

'But, of course, you are only entitled to a judgment against Asemota (Ireland) Ltd if you actually bought your car from them, or if they supplied your car to Wicklow Garages, isn't that so?'

'My Lord,' Derek was on his feet, 'this is a matter of law and not something for the witness.'

The judge agreed with Derek and turned towards me. 'I suggest, Mr McNamara, that you stick to the facts when cross-examining and leave the law to us.'

'Of course, My Lord. Mr O'Connor, what I am really getting at is that Asemota (Ireland) Ltd has no involvement in this case.'

'My Lord ...' Derek was off again.

Before he had a chance to be more specific, His Lordship ruled, 'The facts, Mr McNamara.'

'What I mean is that you did not buy your car from Asemota (Ireland) Ltd. Isn't that so?'

'It is, Mr McNamara,' Mr O'Connor said, adding a little impatiently, 'I have already told you that I bought it from Wicklow Garages.'

'And Asemota (Ireland) Ltd did not supply your car to Wicklow Garages, isn't that so?'

'I have no idea, Mr McNamara, who supplied my car to Wicklow Garages. I simply went into the garage and bought a car. I didn't question them about where they got it. I didn't for a moment think that I would get a car that didn't work or that the garage would go into liquidation or that I would end up here in the witness box. If you make me think about it, it's an Asemota and therefore the garage must have got it from the Asemota company. More than that, I really don't know.'

'Unfortunately, it isn't as simple as that,' I informed the plaintiff.

'Isn't it, Mr McNamara?' enquired Judge Hunter. 'Surely, if the plaintiff bought a defective Asemota – and I am not saying that it is defective – from Wicklow Garages and that company goes into liquidation, the plaintiff is entitled to bring his claim against Asemota?'

'Yes, My Lord, if he identifies the correct Asemota company.'

'I see. I'm sorry for interrupting you, Mr McNamara. Do you have any more questions for this witness?'

'No, My Lord.' The local principal rejoined the plain people of Wicklow.

Derek called his second witness, a mechanical engineer, who dealt one by one with the complaints listed by the plaintiff. It was obvious that this particular

Asemota fell far short of the standard of excellence claimed for it by the manufacturer. Happily, it was not part of my brief to stand over it. Accordingly, I had no questions for the engineer.

It was time for Mr Asemota to take the stand. Even though he had lived in Ireland for upwards of twenty years, he still spoke English as if he had just arrived. For most of that period he had been managing director of Asemota (Ireland) Ltd. He was proud of his company's product and enjoyed spotting his cars as he travelled around the country. If he had a weakness, it was his tendency to be overly precise, to see things too clearly. Black was black and white was white, and there was no such thing as the grey area of the overlap. He had another weakness. He took complaints about his cars too personally.

As he sat in the witness box answering my questions, I had the impression of being in the presence of one who spoke the exact truth. When I had asked him everything I could think of, I resumed my seat, comfortable in the knowledge that the i's had been dotted and the t's crossed. Beyond a shadow of a doubt, the plaintiff's car had been supplied to Wicklow garages by Asemota (UK) Ltd and not by Asemota (Ireland) Ltd. I had a sense that we were on our way to a successful defence of the teacher's claim.

As Derek rose to his feet in the middle of this January afternoon, the snow began to fall heavily outside. 'Mr Asemota, we know that the car was flawed, fundamentally flawed, isn't that so?' Derek opted for a quick score.

'Unfortunately,' replied Mr Asemota.

'So, in essence, what this case comes down to is whether or not Mr O'Connor got this car from you. Isn't that so?'

'It is. That is what the case comes down to. And the answer is he didn't.'

'You are Asemota (Ireland) Ltd and the plaintiff did not buy the car from Asemota (Ireland) Ltd?'

'That is it, as you would say, Mr Delahunt, in a nutshell.'

'From whom do you say the plaintiff bought the car?'

'Wicklow Garages.'

'No, no, no. I know that. From whom do you say Wicklow Garages got the car?'

'Asemota (UK) Ltd.'

'Are you sure?'

'Yes. Unusually.'

'Why do you say "unusually"?'

'Because usually we supplied Wicklow Garages.'

'Was this something of a once off?'

'It was.'

'Mr Asemota,' Judge Hunter intervened, 'is there a relationship between your company Asemota (Ireland) Ltd and Asemota (UK) Ltd?'

'Asemota (Ireland) Ltd is a subsidiary of Asemota (UK) Ltd.'

It was five to four. Phillips, out of breath and with a capping of snow on his head, appeared at my elbow.

'What's happening, Dermot?' he wanted to know.

'We got on early,' I whispered. 'Tell you later.'

'How's it going?'

'I'm not sure. Hunter doesn't seem too interested in corporate structures.'

'I see Mr Phillips in court,' said Hunter. 'I wonder if you could help me, Mr Phillips? Mr Asemota has just told me that his company Asemota (Ireland) Ltd is a subsidiary of Asemota (UK) Ltd.'

'That's quite correct, My Lord.'

'Does your firm act for Asemota (UK) Ltd?'

'Oh yes, My Lord.' Phillips couldn't contain himself. 'We are the Irish solicitors for the entire Asemota Group,' he informed Hunter proudly. He would have been better off keeping his mouth shut.

'Of course Mr Phillips is not acting for Asemota (UK) Ltd in these proceedings as Asemota (UK) Ltd is not a party to the proceedings,' I added, trying to redeem the situation.

'Not until now that is,' Hunter said.

'My Lord?'

'It is very clear to me what I should do in this case. Gentlemen, the evidence is complete I take it?'

Derek and I confirmed that there was no further evidence to be adduced. I knew that somewhere the case had taken an unfavourable turn and sought to make a submission.

'That won't be necessary, Mr McNamara.' The judge's mind was made up. He gave judgment.

'Mr O'Connor is the principal of our local school and works hard for his salary. A motor car is an expensive commodity and a substantial inroad into a teacher's income. Mr O'Connor was entitled to get what he expected, namely, a new car in perfect working order. He didn't get that. Instead, he got a car that was faulty in many respects. In my opinion, he is entitled to his money back.

'Unfortunately for the plaintiff, Wicklow Garages are in liquidation and the question arises – is he entitled to succeed against anyone else? Mr McNamara, an expert in contract law, has come all the way from Dublin to tell me that the plaintiff cannot succeed against Asemota (Ireland) Ltd for the very good reason that that company was not a party to the transaction. Mr McNamara is also an expert in company law, and tells me that Asemota (Ireland) Ltd and Asemota (UK) Ltd are two distinct legal entities and therefore the liability of the English company cannot be visited upon the Irish company. Mr McNamara is very persuasive and, on the basis of what he tells me, I cannot

130

find for the plaintiff.' Light still flickered at the end of the tunnel.

'But that is not the end of the matter,' the judge continued. 'There is one further important piece of information. Mr Phillips very fairly tells me that his firm represents the entire Asemota Group of companies. In that case, I will add Asemota (UK) Ltd as a defendant in this action and, in view of the undisputed condition of the car, give judgment to the plaintiff against that company. I have never been impressed by companies hiding behind corporate structures to avoid their responsibilities.' The sting in the tail.

'The car cost £22,495. I will award damages in that sum. And, of course, costs follow the event. Is there anything else, gentlemen?'

'Tell him he can't do that,' Phillips prompted me.

'Mr Phillips instructs me, My Lord, that we wish to appeal,' was as much as I could rise to.

'Certainly, Mr McNamara. Perhaps you will have better luck in Dublin. And I am sorry you and Mr Phillips were detained so long.'

'Thank you, My Lord.'

The next case was called. Derek gave me a wink as he began to tell the judge what this case was about. We left the courtroom, Phillips repeating 'he can't do that,' not entirely to himself.

In the hallway, it was bitterly cold and bitterly dark. A strip of light above and below the closed door of the courtroom was the only sign of forensic life within. Down the corridor, a shadow or two escaped from the fire-lit comfort of the bar-room and climbed the wall opposite. Outside, where the real world lay, evening vied with the falling snow to engulf the street lights and the shop windows of the closing town.

Phillips, Asemota, Norman and I huddled in a corner of the hallway. Whatever it was about the chill that was at large in Wicklow that evening, it had no interest in taking prisoners. Phillips was furious. It was his first taste of provincial jurisprudence and he wasn't impressed. Having been closeted in Fitzwilliam Square all his professional life, he wasn't able to handle it.

Asemota was more resigned. He never accepted that his car was defective, but Phillips had advised him not to defend the case on that basis and he had gone along with his solicitor's advice. He had got his point across to the judge about the two companies being separate and what that meant for the plaintiff. However, the judge was ahead of him and so Asemota (UK) Ltd was now being dragged across the Irish Sea for the purpose of bailing out the local school principal.

The judgment did not come as a surprise to Norman, who, from the beginning, could see the way the wind was blowing. He was blessed with a sixth sense apparently, though this hadn't deterred him from visiting the judge in chambers. Perhaps if I had accepted the judge's invitation to adjourn the case on account of Mr Phillips's absence, the result might have been happier, he ventured. We had been at a disadvantage without our solicitor, Norman thought, notwithstanding that no one had sought his opinion.

'Could you have adjourned the case, Dermot?' Phillips asked, capitalising on Norman's opening.

'Not really, Mr Phillips.'

'Well, the judge did ask you if you wanted to adjourn the case, Dermot,' Norman contributed prejudicially.

'Did he?' enquired Phillips.

'Well he did and he didn't,' I said.

'Surely, it's one or the other. Either you were offered an adjournment or you weren't.'

'In a literal sense Hunter did offer me an adjournment, but I don't think he intended me to take up the offer. Indeed, when I told him we would go on with the case, he said I had made the right decision.' I was on the point of reminding Phillips that, earlier in the day, I had suggested that he stay in Wicklow rather than return to Dublin. However, I realised just in time that such an observation was unlikely to improve my prospects with Walsh & Phillips. Assistance came from an unlikely place.

'Mr McNamara is right. The judge did not mean it when he offered to adjourn the case. Mr McNamara had no choice,' said Mr Asemota.

I felt a sudden surge of affection for the entire Japanese race and Mr Asemota in particular. Not even Norman with his sixth sense had any inkling of how close Mr Asemota came to having a grateful kiss placed on his cheek. I was off the hook ... for the moment at any rate.

We left the courthouse. Heading down the main street towards our cars, we realised that we would not be getting out of Wicklow that night. There was only one thing for it and that was to book into the Wicklow Arms immediately.

It was a while before Philips was able to leave behind his bewilderment at what the court had just done and a little longer before he tired of telling us how inconvenient it was to be kept out of the office.

I didn't expect Mr Asemota to be a lot of fun – how many funny men have come out of Japan after all? – but once we relaxed a little over a wholesome meal and several glasses of red wine, he entertained us with stories of bringing his car and his culture to more remote parts of our country. As the evening unwound, the distance between our land and his diminished and I felt sure that, in no time at all, I too would be eating noodles and sushi.

133

The nine o'clock news confirmed that this was the heaviest snow-fall in twenty-five years. All around the country, journeys were being abandoned and the B&B business was getting an unseasonal boost.

I still wasn't sure about Norman. Not many devils have the opportunity of sharing a room with their master on their inaugural night of devilling. On balance, I felt that there had been more auspicious beginnings.

Norman continued his analysis of where things had gone wrong and the snow continued to fall on the seaside town outside. I did my best to get to sleep.

THE PINK PALACE AND
THE IVORY TOWER

It was after four on a Monday afternoon in the Library –
time to go home and attack the paperwork – when I heard
my name called.

'Who on earth is looking for me at this hour on a
Monday, Tommy?' I enquired.

'It could only be one person, sir,' Tommy answered,
pointing in the direction of the alcove a short distance
away where the unmistakable towering figure of the
former centre three-quarter J. Arnold O'Reilly stood.
Motionless, like an exhibit that had wandered down from
the Wax Museum, he surveyed the departure of Their
Lordships from the judges' yard.

'Arnold,' I greeted. The exhibit turned in my direction.

'Mac,' he said after a moment. It still wasn't clear that
he was expecting me. Perhaps Tommy was mistaken.

'Were you calling me, Arnold?' I enquired hesitantly.
'Tommy said you were.'

'Oh, well, then I was. Tommy is always right. It was a
few minutes ago and I got distracted watching the judges
heading home at the end of another day. They've a great
life, don't they? Start at eleven, home before the traffic.
I'm seldom out of my office before seven.' I thought better
of telling Arnold why this may be so.

'You're right, Arnold. They're home early every evening,
have free weekends, endless vacations ...' Not to mention
the reserved judgments. 'On the other hand, look at you,

135

in court all day and then back to the office. Letters to write, clients to see … Life just isn't fair, is it, Arnold?' I said, sure that my sympathy would secure my position for another while at least.

'Who said it was, Mac, whoever said it was?' Arnold replied ruefully. 'Time for a coffee?'

'Of course, Arnold.' You refuse coffee with your solicitor at your peril. 'But I'm afraid it will have to be quick. Rachel has a late consultation and I have to collect the children.'

Immediately, Arnold asked after Rachel. 'She's doing very well you know,' he said. 'Very highly thought of on the family side.'

'So she keeps telling me, Arnold.'

'I'm sure she'll be taking silk soon?'

'So she keeps telling me,' I added begrudgingly.

Alice brought us to a table in the corner. The mop was out and the cash was being counted, which was good news from my point of view. Occasionally, if Arnold was not in a hurry, he would unwind totally. Invariably, this meant a trip down memory lane and commentary on the outstanding moments of his rugby career with Trinity. As I neither played rugby nor went to Trinity, I had no interest in this line of reminiscence, but my bank manager said that I owed it to both of us to play my part.

Happily, Arnold's mind was still on the main purpose of his visit to the Law Library that afternoon. 'Liability is in issue,' he said, handing over the ribbonless brief. This was his way of telling me the case was hopeless. I could hear Rachel saying, 'For God's sake, Dermot, get rid of him. For God's sake, get rid of him.' Rachel did not seem to understand the concept of swings and roundabouts. For my part, I still didn't know which were which but, as sure as hell, I had more than my fair share of one of them.

'When is it for?' I asked foolishly.

'Tomorrow, Mac.' It never seemed to occur to him that I might not be available.

'Have I a Senior?' It was, after all, a High Court case.

'Henry Fitzmartin's in town and I have asked him to take the Senior brief.'

'And will he?' I was keen to pin Henry down.

'Of course. Henry always takes my briefs. I wasn't able to speak to him but I left word with his secretary.'

Henry Fitzmartin is a reliable rather than an exciting Silk and, for most Juniors, that is what matters. From all I knew of Henry, if he said he would be there, he would be, but leaving word with his secretary the evening before was hardly a guarantee. Henry was very busy in Europe where, according to himself, he had quite a reputation as a human rights lawyer. All the more reason I felt that he should look after the plaintiff's human rights the following morning.

'I'll never forget that Colours match in the late sixties.' Arnold was off. 'We were leading by a point and, with five minutes to go, we were pinned on our own line. They had the bigger pack and did everything but score.'

Alice will never know the enormity of the favour she did me when, apologetically, she interrupted Arnold at the Havelock Square end. 'Mr O'Reilly, I'm afraid we're closing. It's been a long day. I hope you don't mind.'

'Not at all, Alice,' Arnold said graciously. 'We all have our homes to go to. Pity though. Dermot was just asking me about a famous match I played in many years ago.'

'A pleasure that will have to be postponed, Mr O'Reilly, or would you legal eagles say "adjourned"?' Alice hadn't spent her life in the Four Courts for nothing.

'Adjourned, Alice, that's it,' he chuckled. 'It will have to be adjourned. Maybe until tomorrow when the case is over.'

'That's the spirit, Mr O. You get down here early and you'll have the whole afternoon to yourselves. You can play as many matches as you like.' I was going off Alice.

'Good night, Alice.'

'Good night, Mr O'Reilly. Good night, Dermot. Oh, and good luck with your case tomorrow. I hope you get him off.' Like most members of the public, Alice only recognised the criminal law. If you weren't doing murder cases you weren't a barrister at all.

As we were going up the stairs I asked, 'Consultation, Arnold?'

'Oh certainly, Mac. As usual. Now, let me see. What time should we have it?' I never know why Arnold teases himself with these decisions. There is only one time for a consultation.

'Nine twenty-five, I suppose?'

'See you then, Arnold.'

'No, wait, Mac. Maybe we should say nine twenty ... just in case.' In case of what I was not to find out. Arnold went one way and I the other.

*

'Really, Rachel, I'm not sure that I can take much more of this,' I moaned, pouring my wife a glass of Monday wine. If Rachel thought that I was referring to our marriage, she didn't show it.

'Much more of what, Dermot?' she wanted to know as she settled into the sofa. Rachel's day was done.

'Another unstateable case from Arnold – as usual at the last minute.'

'How often do I have to tell you, Dermot? Dump him.'

'It's not as easy as that, Rachel.'

'It is. Just tell him a few times that you're not available and even he will get the message. Within no time at all he will be attaching his freeloading practice to some other unfortunate and you will be history.'

'That's what I'm afraid of.'

138

'Oh no, I don't mean that. I just mean as far as Arnold is concerned.'

'Yes, I know that, but in fairness he is my best solicitor.'

'So you keep saying, Dermot. But is he? He may brief you but does he pay? Have you ever worked out what he means to you in financial terms?'

'No, I haven't and you're right of course, I should do that. I'll do it this weekend.'

'Anyway, haven't you got that fellow Bartley-Simpson in Fitzwilliam Square?'

'You mean Phillips?'

'Oh, I suppose I do. Haven't you got him in the bag?'

'I'm not sure that "in the bag" is quite the way to put it, but, yes, I have had a few cases for Phillips, and successful too.' However, I didn't think that I could quite look to Phillips as my banker, not for the moment at any rate.

'How was your day?' I asked, changing the subject.

'Exhausting, simply exhausting.' The very thought of it made another sip of wine necessary as she sank deeper into the sofa. 'At least all you guys have to deal with at the end of the day is damages. How much the plaintiff is worth, things like that.'

'That's not unimportant, now, is it?'

'I'm not saying it's not important, but it's not a matter of life and death.'

'Well, nothing is the same since they got rid of the death penalty.'

'There's no need to be facetious, Dermot. You know what I mean. You're not breaking up families and distributing the children, now, are you? Take my case today. I'm acting for an Englishman. His wife is an alcoholic who ran off with another man. You'd think it was a straightforward case, husband entitled to custody. But no. Who do we draw? The most pro-female judge this side of Kabul. "The sacred entitlement of the child to be reared by its mother. Only in the most exceptional circumstances should this be interfered with. And this is not such a circumstance." "What is?" my client wanted to know afterwards and I couldn't tell him. He hadn't a chance. He wasn't even at the races.' Rachel drew breath.

'Sure, Rach. I understand all that. Of course it's heavy jelly emotionally, but that's all there is to it. Social work, that's what it is, not law.'

'It's as much law as what you're at.' Rachel was getting cross.

'And well paid,' I added.

'I'll grant you that, Dermot.' On that note of consensus, recognising the potential for an argument, we headed for a refill and a taste of the cuisine of the evening.

Unfortunately the pheasant was off – in the sense that it was never on – the menu for that Monday evening and we had to make do with a late substitution from the freezer – shepherd's pie – for the third night in a row. If I ever get my hands on the shepherd in question ...

It was on occasions such as this that I had a tendency to mention the fact that my mother loves cooking. Rachel's response is always the same: if she had as much time as my mother she would love cooking too. This was not the night to mention my mother or her cooking. I got on with my shepherd's pie instead.

Dinner over, Rachel headed into *Coronation Street* and I took on Arnold's brief. Thanks to his penchant for less rather than more, that did not take long. I still wasn't in time for Rachel who, even in nodding off, was efficient.

*

The next morning I made it in plenty of time for twenty past nine, while Arnold made it in plenty of time for an hour later. Indeed, having read what I had read the night before, I was surprised that he was there at all. He had a talent for assessing his cases and the 'iffy' ones he left to Samantha, while he went off to something more lucrative. By any yardstick, this was an 'iffy' case and, yet, here he was.

How Christy O'Brien ended up in Arnold's care I was never to find out but, that having happened, Christy could not complain about his representation. His solicitor had assembled a team of substance. A leading consulting engineer was present who was keen to consult with anyone who showed the slightest interest in his photographs of the *locus in quo*. As the distinguished orthopaedic surgeon who would give evidence of Christy's injuries was at that moment distinguishing himself in the operating theatre, he was on standby but could, we were assured, be with us in minutes. Having regard to the seriousness of his injuries, it came as no surprise to Christy that he suffered dreadfully from depression for a considerable spell after the accident, thereby necessitating the attendance of one of the country's foremost psychiatrists. Nor did he think that he would be able to return to the same kind of work, and so a prominent vocational assessor was in the wings to say what sort of work he might be capable of.

The case, on value, was a substantial one. The problem was liability. A substantial case was not much use to the plaintiff unless you could bring it home. Between us all, we knew very little about how Christy's accident had happened. Mr Keogh, the engineer, was well-intentioned and could illuminate the *locus* with his photographs, but that was as far as his illumination could go. Notwith-standing his impressive team of witnesses and, if I may say so, lawyers, much would depend on Christy himself.

Arnold introduced me to Christy. He was a gentleman, softly spoken and spotlessly turned out. From his snow-white shirt and his Sunday suit, I inferred that he regarded the Four Courts as a place worthy of respect. His outfit was completed by a peaked cap, which he removed as we shook hands. He said in a low voice that he was sorry for putting us to all this trouble. I realised immediately that, while his case might be a liability, he himself most definitely was not. He would, I felt sure, commend himself to any reasonable judge.

In the absence of my leader, I was about to take our pre-trial consultation by the scruff of the neck when a disconsolate looking Arnold, who had left us briefly, returned. 'I've bad news, Christy,' Arnold announced solemnly. He proceeded to tell us how Henry never got his message from the previous evening and, as if that wasn't enough, only an hour ago had been invited to act for the defendant. 'It really is a shame, Christy. Mr Fitzmartin is one of our best. It was a rare stroke of luck that I was able to get him last evening.' So much for leaving a message with his secretary. Henry wasn't available and we'd just have to get on with it. 'But not to worry, Christy,' continued Arnold. Christy didn't look in the least worried. 'Mr McNamara is one of our finest Juniors ... sure to take silk soon ... and he'll do a super job for you.'

Time had run out and so my first task on behalf of Christy was to tell Ms Justice Doherty, who was taking the call-over of the personal injuries list in Court 1, that Mr O'Brien's case was 'going on' and likely to take a day. That seemed a reasonable assessment of its duration to me. But not to Henry, who now confirmed that he was indeed acting for the defendant. 'Two days at least, My Lord,' Henry corrected, 'and maybe three.'

Judge Doherty asked me if liability was in issue, and I informed her that I *believed* it was. Henry seemed to take this as a personal insult. 'My friend Mr McNamara knows well that it is, My Lord. And not just that liability is in issue but will be vigorously contested.' The crosser Henry became, the longer he felt the case would take. 'The more I think of it, My Lord, this is a three-day case.' There was only one judge available for a three-day case and so Judge Doherty sent us to Judge Humphries sitting in Court 24 in the roof of the building. Henry looked pleased.

There are those who believe that judges live in ivory towers. Familiarity or otherwise with the inside of a licensed premises might be one way of determining eligibility. In all probability Judge Humphries has never been inside a public house, has never ordered a pint and never heard the words 'Time, gentlemen, please!' bellowed in his ear at closing time. On the contrary, his idea of a night on the town is an early bird in the Fitzwilliam followed by a requiem in the Concert Hall. The ivory tower seemed like his sort of address.

Humphries has been a High Court judge for upwards of twenty years. He is the proud possessor of a razor sharp mind and likes nothing better than to be surrounded by lever-arch files and reported cases. People are not his forte and, *a fortiori*, witnesses are not his forte either. He has been heard to say that the Four Courts would be a far better place without witnesses. In the eternal conflict between principle and people, Humphries always chooses principle.

By definition, personal injury happens to people and not to lever-arch files and, as a result, personal injury cases are heavily reliant upon witnesses, which is why Humphries avoids this area of litigation as best he can. For all these reasons, Mr Justice Humphries was not 'a good draw' for Christy's case.

As the lift was out of order, we climbed the flights of stairs that get steeper and darker the further you rise from Liffey level. Samantha led the way, devouring the steps two at a time. As we climbed, there was no evidence of the time spent by Arnold on the rugby field in his youth. Perspiring profusely, he collapsed on the seat outside Court 24, which was as welcome as any tryline he had ever reached. The plaintiff was no better, which was not surprising given his commitment to The Pink Palace over the years. It was clear that there would have to be a time-out before the consultation could begin.

We were on the top floor at the front of the building looking out on the chilly river. As soon as Christy recovered, I began to put him through his paces. This wasn't an easy task as he had a poor recollection of many of his paces that St Patrick's Day. I did my best to piece together some sort of a jigsaw for presentation to the judge.

According to Christy, he spent the entire of St Patrick's Day two years previously in a hostelry in Rathmines by the name of The Pink Palace, as he did every year. As usual, it was his intention to have one pint and then to travel into town to catch the second half of the parade. He was fiercely proud of being Irish and looked forward to this annual opportunity to wave the flag. Each year, on the eve of the great Fest, he purchased a big bush of shamrock, which he kept by his bed overnight in a jam jar filled with water.

The Pink Palace opened at midday and, at midday on the dot, Christy, covered in shamrock, strode triumph-antly through the portal and took his rightful place on his stool at the counter. Of all days in the year, this was one that Christy took seriously. The first pint of the saint's day was one to savour, particularly as it was on the house. Christy thought it had something to do with Lent. Many Catholics gave up drink for Lent. Not having had a sip since Ash Wednesday meant that the pint of dispensation on St Patrick's Day was all the more delicious.

Christy did not give up drink for Lent, never had. He did not think that religion was about giving things up. But this did not mean that his Patrick's Day pint was any less satisfying. He had a facility for empathising with his fellow man and so, without the hardship of abstention, he shared the reward.

'It's nearly worth giving it up,' Christy's friend on the adjacent stool said as he licked the head of his pint from his lips.

'Def-in-eye-tlee,' Christy echoed, overlooking the fact that it was barely twelve hours since his last pint. It was early in the day for conversation so the two friends contented themselves with silent sipping and sighs of satisfaction.

Christy's eye was on the clock. It was time to get the bus if he was to be in O'Connell Street for the second half of the parade. The day ahead was long and there was plenty of time for as many pints as he might like after the parade.

'Will you go again, Christy?' his friend enquired. 'This one is on me.'

'I will surely,' he replied, his arm well and truly twisted. After all, if he didn't dally over this one he could still catch some of the parade. They watched the barman pull their pints. It really was a highly satisfactory manner in which to begin the celebrations. There they were the two of them, ensconced in friendship in their favourite bar. A shaft of sunlight crept up as far as their high stools. For this year at least, St Patrick had managed to keep the rain, along with the snakes, at bay. Who could blame our hero for settling in?

There wasn't really a defining moment when Christy decided that he would not be going to the parade. It was a decision that evolved. An onlooker, even without knowing the history, would probably have come to the conclusion that Christy was never going to see O'Connell Street. But Christy himself was full of the good intention. It was the middle of the afternoon when he looked at his watch and realised with astonishment that the parade was over a number of hours and that many of the floats were already back in the United States. There and then, he resolved to do things differently the following year.

The Pink Palace was in full flight. St Patrick was undoubtedly man of the match. The gentlemen on the high stools agreed that the ol' sod had come a long way since the fifth century. Celtic tigers were a big improvement on celtic snakes. Christy punched out emotional renditions of 'Hail Glorious St Patrick' and 'Danny Boy'. The saint would have been well pleased with the loyalty of his fans.

It was almost midnight when Christy emerged into the night lights of Rathmines Road, driven by pangs of hunger and a barman keen to hang on to his remaining customers.

I needed a word with Arnold before approaching Henry to see if we could settle.

'What do you think, Arnold?'

'About what, Mac?'

The Grand National, of course.

'The case, Arnold. What do you think of the case? Do you think we'll win?'

'To be perfectly honest, I haven't given it much thought.'

I see.

'I sort of left that to you.'

How convenient.

'Let the dog do the barking, that's what I say, Mac.'

This was news to me. Many the cases where Arnold had had his say, not always wisely. Many the cases where he didn't even seek my advice.

'Well, leaving aside whether or not we will win the case, what do you think it's worth?' I asked.

146

'That's a difficult one, Mac.'

I know that, Arnold. That's why I'm asking you. It is after all a team, isn't it? We are in this together for the benefit of Christy, aren't we?

I was determined not to let Arnold off the hook. 'Were he to succeed in his claim, Arnold, do you think he will be awarded substantial damages or small damages?' Arnold wriggled briefly but then the penny dropped. I was not going away. He was going to have to come up with something. He stretched himself physically at first and then intellectually.

'In my considered opinion, Mac.' This was new territory for Arnold. 'If my client manages to bring his case home in its entirety, then the judge will have no option but to award him substantial damages ...' He paused. 'On the other hand, if he does not do so, then it would seem to follow that his damages will be modest.'

Arnold was surpassing himself. I was sure that he had finished his forecast. But no ... 'Of course, all of this presupposes that he succeeds on liability. Now that is something the judge will have to decide.' Arnold's vast experience was beginning to show. 'I don't have to add that if he loses on liability then he gets nothing.' *Et voilà* – the entire spectrum of possibility in one mouthful. Every eventuality had been covered and I was none the wiser. Arnold stood back as if anticipating a round of applause.

I approached my opposite number. 'One hundred and fifty thousand pounds, Henry,' I threw out as casually as I could. It was every penny of the full value of the case.

'Is that all, Dermot?' Henry wanted to know with that sense of humour that went down so well in Luxembourg. It was Henry's way of telling me that I was out of my depth. Never in my still-short-enough career at the Bar had I asked for such a sum of money. Tens and twenties and thirties, yes, but a hundred and fifty – never. This was a case for a Senior. However, I had pitched and there was no resiling.

'It'll do, Henry,' I replied. 'Of course, you're right. If we bring it home in its entirety he'll get considerably more. But, as you and I know' – I was picking up the patronising bit quite quickly – 'nothing is certain in this business. Pay me one hundred and fifty and the case is as good as dead.'

'I'd love to, Dermot,' Henry lied.

'Well then tell me what you've got, Henry. Humphries is bound to be looking for us soon. We may as well cut to the chase.'

On cue, Humphries' tip-staff appeared in front of us. How like his judge Bartholomew had become. Definitely a chip off the old block. Were the boss to become indisposed, Bartholomew could be propped up on the bench and no one would be the wiser. 'His Lordship was wondering when the parties might be ready to commence.' He even spoke like Humphries.

'Immediately,' Henry replied unhelpfully.

'Oh no, Bartholomew, not yet. Perhaps you could get us a minute or two. We have just started negotiating and you might not be troubled with the case at all.' I was pushing it, I knew.

'In that event I shall inform His Lordship that negotiations have been initiated and that the parties would appreciate a brief indulgence,' Bartholomew announced.

'You will inform His Lordship of no such thing, Bartholomew,' Henry intervened. 'I do not regard these discussions as negotiations and my client certainly does not require time.'

Unlike me, Bartholomew was utterly unruffled by this breakdown in communication between Henry and me. 'Gentlemen, would I be correct in thinking that at this moment in time we are not quite *ad idem*?' he enquired.

'Bartholomew, please ask him for five minutes ... please,' I said.

'Very well, Mr McNamara.' Bartholomew turned on his heels and returned to the judicial den before Henry had a chance to protest.

'Now look, Henry, you're not helping.' It wasn't his fault that Henry wasn't free to lead me, but I was taking it out on him nonetheless. 'Let's make one serious stab at settling this case.' Surely Henry was anxious to get back to posher pastures.

Henry explained to me that he had nothing and that, on this occasion, nothing meant precisely that. 'No one hundred and fifty thousand pounds, no ten thousand pounds to include costs. Nothing.' The driver was furious at being sued. If it hadn't been for his vigilance, the plaintiff would be dead. The driver wanted his costs. I told Henry what I thought of this. Things had reached an impasse.

Bartholomew sensed this immediately upon his return. 'Excuse me for interrupting you, gentlemen, but do I gather that we have not succeeded in resolving our unhappy differences?' he enquired. Henry left him in no doubt. I returned to our alcove.

'That makes things easy,' Samantha said after I explained what had happened. The logic of her observation escaped me.

Arnold was convinced that his old friend Henry had lost the run of himself. 'Europe is doing him no good,' he muttered. 'If you can't rely on your friends to come up with a few bob at the right time then what is the point of briefing them?' Arnold seemed to be getting his ethics in a knot.

We turned and went into court, Samantha going back to pick up Christy who had remained outside.

'O'Brien *v.* Faulkner,' the stern registrar announced.

149

If appearances were anything to go by, and a lot of the time there was little else, this registrar had no appetite for spending his day on a personal injury case. Like his judge above him, he was more at home with probates and liquidations, and the like. No sooner had he made his announcement than his head was buried once again in the backlog of court orders waiting to be drawn up. At least his day would not be a complete waste of time. The judge wanted to know how long the case would take.

'I think it will take a day, My Lord, but Mr Fitzmartin believes that it will take two or perhaps three,' I said.

'Is that so, Mr Fitzmartin?' the judge enquired.

'It is, My Lord.'

'Well, in that case, I have a difficulty gentlemen.' My ears pricked up. 'I am here today and tomorrow but on Thursday I fly to Rio for a judges' conference.' Funny how these conferences always come up during term. 'If the case might go into Thursday, then I can't take it.'

This was good news for Christy sitting quietly at the back of the courtroom. Henry was on his feet immediately. 'Oh, My Lord, perhaps I was a trifle previous with my prediction,' he said. 'On reflection, I am quite confident that Your Lordship will finish the case tomorrow.' Henry was not giving up Humphries without a fight.

'Unfortunately, Mr Fitzmartin, confidence is not enough. I need certainty. I need your guarantees, both of you, that this case will finish tomorrow.'

'You have mine, My Lord,' Henry responded immediately, thereby executing an impromptu u-turn with the ease of a champion ice skater.

'And, of course, Mr McNamara you have always been of the view that the case would finish within two days?'

'I have, My Lord,' I said with regret. Christy had now lost his chance of a transfer to a more sympathetic judge.

'In that case, the sooner we start the better,' the judge said, bringing the preliminaries to an end.

There was no need to tell Humphries anything twice and so, doing my best to avoid repetition, I stuck to the salient facts of the case. For his part, he gave my opening his exclusive concentration and even took a note or two. I was never going to retain the attention of the registrar, who was busy drafting orders. There weren't many people in court. Even if Christy was capable of taking in what was unfolding before him, he was too far from the action to hear what was going on. Immediately in front of him sat our engineer, Mr Keogh, with his magnificent map and photographs proudly set out. Thumbing through his papers, he reminded me of a school boy doing a bit of last-minute revision before an exam. Across from them sat the furious driver of the vehicle and the most important person in court – after the judge himself – the gentleman from the insurance company.

Had a hen party from Henley strayed into the court-room just then, not for a moment would it have mistaken the place for the sort of hotspot it was looking for. Be that as it may, it was my hotspot as I embarked on the pursuit of justice on behalf of Christy.

'Come up, Mr O'Brien,' I said, noticing from the corner of my eye Samantha dashing towards the door. I turned around. Christy was nowhere to be seen. When neither Christy nor Samantha returned, I sought His Lordship's indulgence. 'Might I ask Your Lordship to rise for a few moments?'

'Certainly, Mr McNamara,' Humphries replied obligingly.

'My client does not appear to be in court.' This statement was somewhat euphemistic. Unless Christy was hiding under his seat, it wasn't just a question of appearances. He was not in court. 'Mr O'Reilly assures me that he was present while I was opening his case to Your Lordship.'

'Perhaps he became unwell, Mr McNamara. If you would be good enough to inform my crier when you are ready to proceed.'

'Thank you, My Lord.'

'Is that all right, Mr Fitzmartin?'

'My Lord.'

With that, the judge returned to whatever probates and liquidations were awaiting him in his chambers.

Arnold took off after Samantha. In the meantime I had another go at Henry but to no avail. As far as he was concerned, Christy's disappearance was not a surprise and he might not be back. The registrar was revelling in this opportunity for order drafting. I was almost alone in the courtroom.

Samantha returned some minutes later with Christy. 'He's very nervous,' she said as she told me quickly where she had found him.

She had followed her hunch down the stairs to the public bar in the basement. Christy had been in the act of raising the pint of dark stuff to his aroused lips when she cruelly intercepted it. 'It'll have to wait, Christy,' she said in a kindly voice, as if understanding his need.

'Just a sip surely, Samantha,' he pleaded before yielding and, like a child, following Samantha upstairs.

I called Christy to the witness box yet again. He took the Bible in his nervous hand and repeated the oath after the registrar.

'Sorry, sir,' he said quietly to the judge before taking his seat.

'That's alright, Mr O'Brien. No harm done. You just sit down there and answer your counsel's questions,' said the judge, who would not in a million years have guessed the true whereabouts of Christy during those missing minutes.

'Mr O'Brien, I think you're the plaintiff in this action. Isn't that so?' There were not many in court and no one doubted that Christy was the plaintiff, nonetheless I felt obliged to ask the conventional opening question. Christy himself of course had no idea what I was talking about.

'If you say so, sir,' Christy replied compliantly.

'You can take it, Mr O'Brien, that you are the plaintiff,' reassured the judge.

'Thank you, sir.' Christy fingered his cap, which he had placed on the ledge in front of him.

'Mr O'Brien, may I ask you if you recall St Patrick's Day two years ago?'

'You may, sir,' Christy replied quietly and precisely.

'Well, do you?' I asked him when he failed to go on to the second part of his answer.

'I do,' he replied, 'in a manner of speaking.'

'What exactly do you mean "in a manner of speaking"?'

'Well, sir, it's like this. When the car hit me I got a blow to my head and the result is that my memory is ... how would you say ... interspersed.'

'"Interspersed", Mr O'Brien?' asked the judge, who was interested in language.

'Well, I remember some parts of the day, sir, and not others,' Christy clarified.

'I see. Thank you. Sorry, Mr McNamara.'

'Not at all, My Lord. Mr O'Brien, you say that a car hit you. Perhaps you could assist the court by telling us what you remember of the day before the car hit you.'

'I can, sir. It's really quite simple because I don't remember a whole lot. I remember early on St Patrick's Day going into The Pink Palace in Rathmines for a drink before going into town for the parade. I remember leaving The Palace that night and I have very little recollection of what happened in between.'

'How very convenient,' Henry muttered under his breath.

'I'm sorry, Mr Fitzmartin, did you say something?' enquired the judge.

'No, My Lord,' Henry lied.

'Well, Mr O'Brien, perhaps you could tell us about leaving The Pink Palace?' I continued.

'Well, sir, suddenly I felt very hungry and wanted a feed of chips and so I left the pub and headed for my local chipper.'

'If I pass you Mr Keogh's map you might be able to point out to His Lordship where The Pink Palace and the chipper are?' I said, at the same time indicating to Arnold to hand one of Mr Keogh's maps to the witness.

'I'm not much use with maps. Wouldn't know me north from me south. I'm sorry,' Christy said, turning towards the bench.

'That's alright,' the judge replied. 'Many of us can't read maps. I'm sure we will be able to follow your journey from The Pink Palace to the chip shop.'

'Thank you, sir,' said Christy. 'I'm sure you know The Pink Palace anyhow. It's quite a landmark in Rathmines and everyone knows it.'

'I'm afraid I don't,' the judge replied. 'You are finding out, Mr O'Brien, that judges do not know everything.' Henry nodded agreement.

'Indeed I am.' Christy sounded disappointed. 'Are you from Rathmines, sir?' he asked and was relieved to learn that His Lordship was not. This was something by way of mitigation at least.

'From Rathgar, in fact, Mr O'Brien,' said Humphries, doing his best to distance himself from his ignorance.

'And you don't know The Pink Palace, sir?' Christy wasn't letting him off that lightly. 'Well, at least if you're from Rathgar you'll definitely know Comans?'

154

'From a little outside Rathgar actually, Mr O'Brien,' Humphries said, as if he lived in West Cork. 'Perhaps we should get back to Rathmines and The Pink Palace.'

'Well, sir, if you travel down from Comans ... I mean Rathgar, in the direction of town, you come to Rathmines Road. At Madigan's ...' Christy glanced at the judge and then made an alteration to his directions. 'Just beyond the Garda Station you turn left ... into the straight as it were, and travel along Rathmines Road.' The wind was now behind Christy and he thought he might test His Lordship again. 'The Rathmines Inn, sir?' he enquired.

'I'm afraid not, Mr O'Brien.'

'The Four-Faced Liar?'

'Now I'm with you ... the clock half way down Rathmines Road on the right?' Humphries was pleased with this breakthrough.

'Well, just beyond that is The Pink Palace.'

'At last,' said Humphries. 'I'm beginning to feel a bit thirsty myself. Now, Mr McNamara, you might like to take up the running again.'

'Thank you, My Lord,' I said, turning towards my witness. 'Mr O'Brien, you told us that you recall leaving The Pink Palace?'

'I did.'

'What did you do then? Where did you go?'

'Well, as I said, I was starving. It had been a long day.' Christy made it sound as if he had been breaking boulders. 'And I wanted a bag of chips. Often on the way home I call into Bocelli's.'

'Please tell His Lordship where Bocelli's is.'

'Certainly I will.' He looked at the judge. 'You come out of The Palace and you walk in the direction of town as far as O'Reilly's. Do you know where O'Reilly's is?' This time Christy turned towards me.

'I confess I do,' I said, as His Lordship pleaded ignorance for the umpteenth time.

'Well, for the benefit of Sir I can tell you that it is a good bit down on the same side.'

'As far as the church?' Humphries wanted to know.

'Not so far,' Christy replied. 'I remember reaching O'Reilly's, which is across the road from Bocelli's, and that's as much as I remember until I woke up in the ambulance to the sound of the siren.'

'Do you recall being hit by a car? Do you recall the car?' I asked.

'I don't. I remember being on the footpath about to cross and next I was in the ambulance.'

'And the car, Mr O'Brien, in which direction was the car travelling? Towards town or out of town?' His Lordship enquired.

'I can't say, sir. I never saw the car.'

'From town, My Lord,' Henry interjected.

'Do I understand your case correctly, Mr O'Brien?' the judge asked. 'You were on the footpath opposite Bocelli's waiting to cross Rathmines Road. As you crossed the road, you were struck by a car coming from town.'

'Indeed you do, sir. Most correctly. Mr O'Reilly told me before I came in here that it was very important that you got everything.'

'Very wise of Mr O'Reilly. Indeed, Mr O'Brien, I have been travelling up and down Rathmines Road on foot and by car for many years and I feel I know it better now than ever before.'

'Thank you,' Christy replied appreciatively.

That was as much as Christy could contribute to the circumstances of the accident. I took him through his injuries and finally asked him what he thought of his chances of getting back to work.

'Not great, to be honest, not great.'

Detecting, as I thought, the slightest raising of a judicial eyebrow, I decided to leave well enough alone and release Christy to Henry's best endeavours. It was not the strongest of cases, but so far it had gone as well as it might.

Henry Fitzmartin, S.C. rose to his feet. 'Would you be good enough, Mr O'Brien, to inform the court of the time of your accident?' he asked.

'I'm afraid I can't, sir,' replied Christy apologetically.

'Why can't you?'

'Because I don't know.'

'Well, in general terms, could you tell us if it was morning, noon or night?'

'It was night, well and truly night.' Christy was anxious to help.

'So, it was night and dark when you left The Pink Palace and wandered up Rathmines Road.'

I was on my feet immediately. 'I object, My Lord, to my friend's use of the word "wandered".'

'Certainly, and so you should. Mr Fitzmartin?'

'Very well, My Lord, I will rephrase my question. Mr O'Brien, it was dark and night when you left the pub and walked up Rathmines Road?'

'It was, yes.'

'And could you be a little more precise? For example, could it have been midnight?'

'It could, but I really don't know for sure.'

'Mr Faulkner, who was driving the car which you walked out in front of ...'

Once again I was on my feet, but Humphries did not need to hear me. 'Mr Fitzmartin, I have to ask you to restrain yourself. You know the rules of evidence. They may be more relaxed in Luxembourg, but we are not in Luxembourg now,' the judge said.

157

'If it please Your Lordship,' Henry said in an untroubled tone, as if the judge had been paying him a compliment. 'Mr Faulkner will say the accident happened at midnight, Mr O'Brien.'

'And if he does, sir, I cannot disagree.'

Henry then wanted to know at what time Christy had gone to The Pink Palace. 'Could it have been eight o'clock?' he asked.

'Oh no. This isn't an early morning house. It couldn't have been that early.'

'I didn't mean eight in the morning. Eight in the evening.'

'No, sir, it was earlier than that.'

'Six, Mr O'Brien?'

'I'd say earlier, sir.'

'Three?'

'Earlier.'

'Twelve? Opening time is twelve. Was it twelve, Mr O'Brien?'

'More than likely, sir. I was just going in for one before the parade ... as I do every year.'

'So you had one and then went to the parade. At what time did you get back to The Pink Palace?'

'I didn't go to the parade.'

'You didn't go to the parade?'

'No, I never ...'

'Never left The Pink Palace?'

'Exactly.'

Henry paused to do some sums and resumed. 'Would I be exaggerating if I said that you had been in The Pink Palace for twelve hours before this accident occurred?'

'You could be right, sir. I haven't actually worked it out, but you could be right.'

'And during those twelve hours in The Pink Palace, Mr O'Brien, what were you doing?'

'I was having a drink, sir.'

'One drink?'

'No, sir. Not one drink. Not in twelve hours.'

'Well then how many, Mr O'Brien?'

'Oh, I couldn't tell you that. I wasn't counting. It was St Patrick's Day,' Christy said.

'Well, let me help you, Mr O'Brien. Would it have been twelve pints, a pint an hour?'

'Oh no, sir, not twelve pints,' Christy was put out by this slur on his drinking capacity. 'More like two pints an hour.'

'Twenty-four pints then, Mr O'Brien, would that be it?'

'Yes, sir,' Christy said, happier with this estimate.

'In summary then, Mr O'Brien, we can say that between midday and midnight you consumed twenty-four pints of ...?'

'Guinness, sir.'

'Twenty-four pints of Guinness, is that so?'

'Give or take.' Christy replied, not wanting to be tied down.

'That's three gallons of Guinness that you consumed on St Patrick's Day,' Henry informed him.

'Was it really?' Christy asked with pride.

'What about food, Mr O'Brien? Did you eat anything during the day?' Henry moved on, confident that Christy's excessive consumption of alcohol wasn't lost on the judge.

'Oh loads of sangers. Ham and mustard sangers go down a treat with Uncle Arthur. Fresh bread, thick slices of ham and a layer of mustard together with a pint of Guinness. There's nothing quite like it.'

'I'm sure there isn't, Mr O'Brien. How many sandwiches "went down", as you put it, with "Uncle Arthur"?'

'Oh loads, sir, loads.'

'Do you think you could be more precise?'

'Well, let me think ... let me see ... I'd say I had one about three ... maybe another at about six ... and perhaps a third at about nine ... yes, I'd say that's probably right.'

'Three sandwiches in all, is that correct?'

'Give or take, give or take.'

'Mr O'Brien, when you stepped out of The Pink Palace at midnight you had just completed a twelve-hour shift during which you had consumed three gallons of Guinness and three ham and mustard sandwiches. Is that a fair summary?'

'It is, sir, give or take.' Christy was a little taken aback by Henry's astonishment.

'I have to put it to you, Mr O'Brien, that you were under the influence of alcohol when you left the pub?' Henry was full of the high moral ground. It didn't faze Christy, who had a different perspective.

'I have to agree with you, sir. Def-in-eye-tlee,' Christy said proudly.

'Not to put a tooth in it, Mr O'Brien, you were drunk.'

'Oh no, sir, I wasn't drunk,' Christy replied, indignantly. 'Under the influence maybe. Drunk – never.'

'There's a difference, Mr O'Brien?' Henry asked.

'Yes indeed, sir. It would take a lot more than that to make me drunk.' Those in court laughed.

'I'm inclined to agree with Mr O'Brien,' His Lordship interrupted, looking at Henry.

'That it would take more than twenty-four pints to make him drunk, My Lord?'

'No, Mr Fitzmartin, that he makes a distinction between being drunk and being under the influence.'

'Is Your Lordship serious?' Henry asked. He was surprised by His Lordship's alignment on this issue. Like the rest of us, he had assumed that Humphries was a poor draw for the plaintiff.

'Always, Mr Fitzmartin,' said Humphries. I was inclined to believe him.

'Is Your Lordship saying that it is acceptable as a matter of law to be wandering around city streets when one is drunk?' Henry sought clarification of His Lordship's jurisprudence in relation to alcohol.

'My Lord ...' I tried in vain to get in.

'It's alright, Mr McNamara. No, Mr Fitzmartin, I'm saying no such thing. I'm saying no more than to be drunk and to be under the influence is not always one and the same.' The judge paused.

'My Lord ... "wandering around the streets" ... my friend ...' I tried for a second time.

'That's all right, Mr McNamara. I have your point and you needn't worry. There is no such evidence ... not so far anyhow. Please proceed, Mr Fitzmartin.'

'Mr O'Brien, in the condition you were in, you stepped off the pavement and into the path of Mr Faulkner's car, isn't that so?' continued Henry.

'If you say so, sir. I have no memory. I don't know how the accident happened,' Christy said.

'Giving Mr Faulkner no opportunity to avoid colliding with you, isn't that so, Mr O'Brien?'

'If you say so, sir. I just don't know.'

It didn't take all of Henry's experience at home and abroad to know when to sit down. He could be accused of being pleased with his journey so far. There was no denying the fact that on the night Christy had 'drink on him'. As for the accident, it did seem that he had stepped out onto Rathmines Road en route to his chips, giving the driver no chance to slow down or stop.

The omens were in Henry's favour.

I called Mr Keogh, our engineer. We spent some time looking at his award-winning photographs. The accident location turned out to be highly photogenic and so he had photographed it from every angle and in every light. Mr Keogh had fulfilled his obligation to the court with meticulous diligence and deserved the accolade from the bench. This was a straight stretch of roadway, well lit at night so that, from either party's perspective, there was an unimpeded view for upwards of a football pitch. It may have been that everyone in court knew this without Mr Keogh's assistance, but with his assistance we certainly knew it better.

'It's almost one o'clock, Mr McNamara,' the judge observed, looking at the mahogany clock that had been forever five minutes fast. The sacred hour of luncheon. The judge may have been keen to get to Rio, but he wasn't going on an empty stomach.

'Shall we say two fifteen?'

'If it please Your Lordship,' Henry and I responded in unison. As it obviously did.

'Is there any need for me to stay, Mr McNamara?' Christy wanted to know when we met after lunch.

'Oh, I think you'd better, Christy. After all, it's your case,' I advised. 'And of course you never know when the judge might want to ask you some more questions.'

I hoped that this contingency would not arise as, undoubtedly, the pints that Samantha had saved Christy from at eleven had been consumed over lunch. Another rendition of 'Hail Glorious St Patrick' was definitely on the cards. Just before the refreshed judge emerged from his chambers, I checked to see if Christy had taken my advice. He had and was now accepting some peppermints from Samantha at the back of the court.

'Unfortunately, my medical witnesses will not be available until tomorrow,' I informed the judge when he returned.

'That is if you need them at all,' Henry interjected.

'I beg your pardon, Mr Fitzmartin?' said Humphries.

'Oh nothing, My Lord. I was just trying to assist my friend,' replied my opponent.

'That's alright, Mr McNamara. Have you any other liability witnesses to be going on with?' Humphries continued.

'In fact, My Lord, that's my case except for the medical evidence,' I said.

'Very good then. Mr Fitzmartin, I think we should leave the medical evidence until the morning – indeed you might be able to agree the medical reports overnight – and in the meantime maybe you would call your evidence? Does that present you with any difficulty?'

'None at all, My Lord.'

'Well then, if you would be so good as to call your witnesses, we might get closer to our destination.'

When it comes to litigation, it is never too late to learn. Usually, you know at the outset what your client's account of the accident is and you wait with interest for what the defendant will say. However, in this instance, the defendant was making his way to the witness box and I still had no idea how the accident had happened.

It was clear immediately that Mr Faulkner was indignant at being blamed for Christy's accident. He had been in Dublin for the St Patrick's Day celebrations and, sober as His Lordship, was making his way to his brother's house in Rathfarnham. He agreed with Henry that he was no stranger to the area. There had been nothing excessive about his speed and there was nothing to distract him from the job in hand. All of a sudden, Mr O'Brien stepped from the footpath and into his life, giving him no say whatever in the matter. His questioning of the witness over, Henry resumed his seat in the front bench.

I rose to my feet with no idea at all of how to begin my cross-examination of the indignant defendant. At this point my case looked hopeless. How could I rescue it? How could I show that Mr Faulkner was driving too fast or that he should have seen Christy sooner? I needed something – anything – to make the witness liable.

I didn't expect to receive much inspiration from Arnold's note. Two words – 'Reg. No.' I had no idea what he meant and was about to crumple the note when I remembered that I still did not have an opening question. I decided to delve deeper. 'What do you mean, Arnold?'

Looking at me as if I was being more than usually slow, he replied, 'Speed'. I was none the wiser. I did as the note said and checked the registration number in Mr Keogh's photographs: 'JIW 7965' on a yellow number plate. Suddenly I realised what Arnold was getting at. I didn't think much of it, but I didn't have an alternative.

'Mr Faulkner, as you said, you were visiting Dublin. Isn't that right?'

'Yes,' the defendant answered in a clipped manner.

'Something you do from time to time, is that so?'

'Yes.'

'Coming from?'

'Belfast.'

'And what brings you to Dublin? Rugby internationals, I suppose?'

'Yes, and every Patrick's Day my brother and his wife, who live in Rathfarnham, throw a party.'

'And is that why you were down on this occasion?'

'Yes.'

'Were you on your way to the party?'

'Yes. I should have been down earlier in the day but something cropped up in the office and I was detained. Were it not for the fact that it was also their silver wedding anniversary, I mightn't have bothered.'

'What time did you leave Belfast?' I asked.

'My Lord,' Henry interrupted, 'what on earth has this to do with an accident that took place in Rathmines?'

'*De bene esse*, Mr Fitzmartin.' I had to admit that Humphries was giving Christy every chance.

'Mr Faulkner?' I continued.

'About ten o'clock,' he replied.

'In the evening, Mr Faulkner?' I enquired, just to be sure.

'Yes.'

'You left Belfast at ten in the evening and at midnight you were on the south side of Dublin, more than one hundred miles down the road. Is that so, Mr Faulkner?'

'It is.'

I paused to allow this fact to sink in. 'You were travelling too fast when this accident occurred, isn't that so, Mr Faulkner?'

'No, it is not,' the witness replied, cold as a Belfast Sunday.

'How are you so definite?'

'Because I was travelling in a built-up area where there is a 30 miles per hour speed limit and I have a thing about speed limits.'

'What sort of a thing do you have about speed limits, Mr Faulkner?'

'I observe them, Mr McNamara.'

'And when you were on the open road between Belfast and Dublin, were you observing them?'

'Certainly.'

'Like your fellow countrymen, Mr Faulkner?'

'What do you mean, Mr McNamara?'

'Isn't it well known that northerners drive too fast, particularly down here?'

'My Lord,' Henry interrupted, 'surely my friend is not suggesting that if someone from Northern Ireland is involved in an accident, it can be assumed that he is driving too fast?'

'Mr McNamara, you're not saying that, are you?' Humphries asked. I suppose I was really. 'Are you saying I should take judicial notice of the fact that northerners drive too fast?' the judge continued unsympathetically.

'In a nutshell, My Lord.'

'And therefore?'

'And therefore there is a strong likelihood that Mr Faulkner was driving too fast at the time of this accident, particularly when we know he was so late for his brother's party.'

'You're not serious, Mr McNamara?' Humphries wanted to know, eyebrows raised.

'I am, My Lord,' I replied stubbornly. I had nothing else.

'Citizens of Northern Ireland drive fast. Therefore Mr Faulkner is responsible for this accident. Is that what you are asking me to find?' Humphries was oversimplifying.

'Not quite, My Lord.'

'Well, thank goodness for that, Mr McNamara. Please proceed.' I had gone as far as I could really.

'Mr Faulkner, had you not been in such a hurry to get to the party, you would have been able to take avoiding action when Mr O'Brien stepped off the path?'

'No. Emphatically no. Mr O'Brien gave me no chance.'

I sat down, thinking that was probably that. Surely Henry wouldn't bother calling any more witnesses. Surely Humphries could come to only one conclusion.

To my surprise, Henry called the Garda. In her navy-blue uniform, she was pretty, precise and predictable, and added nothing to the tableau that was already before His Lordship. I could think of nothing worthwhile to ask her. However, mountains are there to be climbed and witnesses exist to be examined and so I referred her to her sketch-map. I was only going through the motions.

'Garda, you have marked on your sketch-map where the point of impact was?'

'That's correct. It's where I have put an "X".'

'And what makes you think that that was the point of impact?'

'Because you will see from the map that that was where the debris was,' she said.

'I see. Thank you. And that is on the defendant's correct side of the road, isn't that so?'

'It is.'

'Garda, it could be that the accident happened on the driver's incorrect side of the road but the debris didn't fall until the car was back on its correct side, isn't that so?'

Henry was up immediately. 'Pure speculation, My Lord.'

'I couldn't answer that, My Lord,' the Garda replied.

I left it. 'Garda, one final question, what did the debris consist of?'

'The usual. Some mud and some glass.'

'Is that all?'

'Yes,' she said as she looked over her notebook, 'that's all.' I resumed my seat. Then, looking again, she added, 'Oh, and I see here I have written in brackets "a bag of chips".'

I was on my feet immediately. 'A bag of chips? I see.' I paused. 'Why in brackets?'

'I didn't know if the chips had anything to do with Mr O'Brien. After all, they may have been there already.'

'Thank you, Garda.'

This was just what we needed – a lifeline.

The judge thanked and released the Garda. Henry confirmed that that was his case. The judge announced that he would take my medical evidence the following morning. Bartholomew commanded all to rise and, in case the few in court had not heard what his judge said, repeated that the court would sit again at eleven the following day.

We regrouped briefly outside the courtroom. There wasn't any point in talking to Christy who was, of course, oblivious to the end-of-day development in the case. Arnold had an important visit to make and so we went our separate ways.

At nine twenty-five that night the phone rang. An excited Arnold. 'We're in business,' he said.

He wouldn't say any more over the phone, but would see me in the morning along with Signor Bocelli, the proprietor of the chip shop.

*

The next morning, Arnold arrived on time for once. He introduced Bocelli. Signor Bocelli had come to Ireland with his family when he was ten years of age. He met Arnold on the rugby field and they became friends. They had played many matches against one another and Arnold, who lived nearby, liked nothing better than to drop in for a bag of chips and a chat about those very matches. I listened to what he had to say about Christy's accident.

At eleven o'clock, I was addressing Humphries. 'I agree respectfully with Your Lordship and reluctantly with Mr Fitzmartin, it is an unusual application. I ask Your Lordship not to refuse my application simply because it is unusual.' There were judges who would take the easy option.

'I will not do that,' the judge said. 'In fact, I will go further. I will accede to your application, Mr McNamara, but I do so *de bene esse*. Do you understand?'

'I do, My Lord. May it please Your Lordship.'

I called my surprise witness.

'Mr Bocelli, you are the proprietor of a fish and chip shop on Rathmines Road, is that correct?' I asked.

'I am,' Bocelli replied.

'Do you recall St Patrick's night two years ago?'

'I do.'

'Where were you?'

'I was in my shop. St Patrick's night is one of our busiest nights. Irish people like a bag of chips after their pints.'

'Do you recall an accident occurring on the road outside your shop?'

'I do.'

'Did you see it?'

'I did.'

'What did you see?'

'I saw Christy crossing the road and being struck by a car.'

'Did you do anything?'

'No, I did not. We were very busy at the time and a lot of passers-by went to Christy's assistance.'

'Do you know Mr O'Brien?'

'I do. He's a regular.'

'Where was the car coming from?'

'From town. Travelling from left to right as I looked out my window.'

'And where on the roadway was it?'

'As far as I could see it was on the correct side of the road.'

'And can you say anything about its speed?'

'No, except to say that I did not think that it was travelling fast. In fact, there was quite a bit of traffic on the road and also quite a number of pedestrians crossing it – it was just after closing-time – and he couldn't have been travelling too fast.'

I could sense Humphries becoming impatient. 'Just one more question.' I paused. 'From which side was Mr O'Brien crossing?'

'Oh, my side of course. He had just been in for his bag of chips. Christy is a creature of habit. A few pints in The Palace, a bag of chips in my place and then back across the road and on home.'

'Are you certain of this, Mr Bocelli?' Humphries asked with renewed interest.

'Quite certain, Judge. It's the same routine every night. In fact, I remember that night he said something about not getting to the parade.'

'Thank you,' I said to Bocelli and sat down.

How quickly things can change. Once again Judge Humphries was giving the case his full attention. Even the registrar looked up. It was Henry's turn to wriggle.

'Mr Bocelli, could you please tell the court when you were first asked to give evidence in this case?' Henry asked with great deliberation.

'Certainly, eh, Mr ...'

'Fitzmartin.'

'Last evening, Mr Fitzmartin.' Arnold was nodding agreement.

'And could you tell the court in what circumstances you were asked to give evidence?' Henry continued.

'Of course, Mr Fitzmartin,' Bocelli said courteously. 'About eight o'clock, Arnold called in on his way home. I assumed he was going to have something to eat and a bit of a chat, as he always does. But last night was different. He was in a hurry and was agitated. No time for chips or chat. He only asked me two things.'

'And what were they, Mr Bocelli?'

'He wanted to know if I had seen Christy's accident and if I knew which way he was crossing the road at the time.'

170

'And what did you tell him?'

'I told him exactly what I told you. That's all he wanted to know and he was gone. He rang me later, just before twenty-five past nine, to find out if I could come to court this morning.' Arnold's nodding was seemingly unstoppable.

'And did you speak to him again about the accident?'

'No. Not a word. I had a quick word with Christy's barrister of course ... Mr ... eh ...'

'Can you explain, Mr Bocelli, how it is that you were only approached last evening for the first time to give evidence in this case?'

'I can't. You will have to ask Arnold about that.'

'And you never came forward yourself at the time of the accident?'

'No, I didn't. Perhaps I should have, but we were very busy at the time and there were plenty of people around.'

'And of course Mr O'Reilly and Mr O'Brien are friends of yours?'

'Arnold has been a very good friend for many years and Christy is a very good and loyal customer,' Signor Bocelli answered openly.

Fair procedures meant that Henry was allowed to recall Mr Faulkner to see what he had to say about this *de bene esse* evidence.

'I really don't know,' Mr Faulkner said. 'I assumed all along that he stepped off the footpath from my left and into my path. I didn't see him until the accident happened. Had he been coming from the other side of the road, I would surely have seen him,' the defendant continued with suicidal honesty.

'And isn't that the point, Mr Faulkner?' I asked when my turn came. 'Mr O'Brien was crossing from your right. He was more than halfway across the road when he was struck. You ought to have seen him?'

'All I can say is that I didn't see him and, therefore, I assumed he came from the footpath.' Mr Faulkner accelerated towards the gallows and I resumed my seat.

I called my doctors. After Signor Bocelli, their evidence was received with greater interest. There was no need for Mr Justice Humphries to rise for a few moments to put his thoughts in order before giving his judgment.

'This case has been something of a learning curve for me,' the judge confessed. 'And certainly Rathmines will never be the same again. In particular, if I ever need a pint or a bag of chips, I will know where to go and I now regard myself as something of an expert on the public houses on either side of the Four-Faced Liar.

'For a long time this case looked hopeless from Mr O'Brien's point of view. He was unable to point to anything negligent in Mr Faulkner's driving and, in addition, if not drunk, was under the influence of alcohol. He had con-sumed three gallons of Guinness, give or take, in the course of his twelve hours of celebration. On that evi-dence, I could not in conscience have found for Mr O'Brien.

'Overnight, *a deus ex machina* as it were, Mr Bocelli comes before me. Like Mr Fitzmartin, I was suspicious. How could he arrive so late? I listened carefully to his evi-dence and to Mr Fitzmartin's forceful cross-examination. I was particularly impressed by the calm manner in which Mr Bocelli gave his evidence. Having heard and observed him, I have no doubt at all that, as he says, Mr O'Brien was crossing the road from the chip shop to the other side, in other words from Mr Faulkner's right. This evidence is crucial to the liability in this case. Without it, Mr O'Brien must lose. With it, he must win.

'However, it is clear from the circumstances of the accident that Mr O'Brien is more at fault. Therefore, I will apportion liability 75 per cent/25 per cent in favour of the defendant. I assess damages at £80,000. Were I to accept the evidence relating to future loss of earnings, the damages would be considerably higher. However, I think that if Mr O'Brien does not get back to work, it will not be entirely due to his injuries. There will be judgment for the plaintiff for £20,000.'

I asked for my hard-won costs. 'Of course,' Humphries confirmed. He returned Mr Keogh's photographs to Arnold along with other exhibits that he had accumulated during the hearing. 'In view of my travel commitments tomorrow, I will not take up any further cases,' he announced to anyone who might be interested, including the stern registrar who brightened at the prospect of a half day.

'May I take the opportunity to wish Your Lordship a safe journey,' I said sycophantically, but I couldn't help myself. Humphries thanked me and left the bench to pack his bags for Rio. Henry was in a corner with Mr Faulkner as we left the room.

Arnold was over the moon. In fairness, he was entitled to be. In the time I had known him, not once had he shown a hint of the alertness he had displayed in this case. Whether it was the bags of chips over the years or his friendship with Bocelli, something in Arnold had been ignited and we all were the beneficiaries.

Needless to say, Christy had no idea what was going on. He took Samantha aside and asked her the result. She told him that he was twenty grand better off. He understood that alright. One by one, he shook us by his grateful hand and thanked us profusely. Then he headed off in the direction of The Pink Palace to spend as much of his twenty grand as quickly as he could.

Arnold was keen to have a detailed postmortem, so down we went to the restaurant. We revisited every nook and cranny of the case, which we agreed had indeed looked hopeless. We toasted the Garda and her bag of chips in brackets. Bocelli was full of admiration for the job that had been done on behalf of his loyal customer. No one mentioned that Bocelli might have been identified earlier but, to be fair to Arnold, the one consistent instruction in the case had been that Christy was on his way to buy his chips.

Eventually, even Arnold tired of analysing the case. He turned to his rugby pal and together they swerved and sidestepped their way through the mists of ancient matches. The memories of this ageing pair held little interest for me and even less for Samantha. Her stick of chewing-gum must have been well worn out by the time our elders resurfaced.

'One against the head,' Arnold said to Bocelli as we parted.

I couldn't wait to get home that evening to tell Rachel about the win. She muttered something about swallows and summer as she sipped her gin and tonic.

Behind the door of his ivory tower Humphries was getting ready for his trip. And no doubt Christy was already in full voice in The Pink Palace.

THE APPEAL

'Shall I begin at the beginning?' Professor Moriarty wanted to know, his obsession with origins unresolved.

'Where else?' Margaret replied.

We were in Arnold's office in Lower Gardiner Street on the eve of the professor's appeal from the Circuit Court the previous October. Immediately after that defeat, Arnold said he would appeal and bring in Margaret. Here we were then, in fulfilment of Arnold's plan, to brief Margaret Thompson, S.C. fully on the case.

If Margaret was in any way offended by the untidiness of Arnold's office, she didn't show it. Choosing the only comfortable chair in the room after Arnold's, she seemed utterly at home as she commenced the consultation.

I had rarely seen Arnold so relaxed. Like a fish out of water when you met him in the Four Courts, in Gardiner Street he was well and truly restored to his natural habitat. He sat in a high-backed, black leather swivel chair, the buttons on each arm of which permitted him to swivel in all directions, at several angles and a range of speeds. Directly facing him was a grandfather clock that chimed loudly on the half-hour. The chime was Arnold's cue to interrupt the consultation for the exhortation, 'We must win this case, Margaret.' That said, Arnold, happy as a child in a chair-o-plane, pressed the buttons and off he went.

The professor and Samantha took the remaining chairs and I was left with a wall to lean against. I did my best to avoid standing on original title deeds spread out on the floor. I could see Arnold in the rugby photograph on the wall behind him. Moriarty didn't look like a rugby player, but I wondered if by any chance he might be in it too. I tried to pick him out.

Through the open door, I could see Arnold's salty secretary poised to pick up her plastic bag as soon as the grandfather clock struck five and flee the premises. Any member of the public or the profession seeking to detain her a moment beyond five would do so at his peril.

Margaret is a rising star of the Inner Bar. She hasn't taken silk long but has already made her mark. When God made Margaret he was in excellent form and, when it came to dishing out the talents, he lost the run of himself. There is no asset she does not have in abundance – looks, confidence, intelligence.

Perhaps sensing the mild-looking professor might need encouragement to tell his story, she said, 'Professor Moriarty, I would like you to know that all of us are here for one purpose and one purpose only and that is to make sure that your case is presented in the best manner possible tomorrow. You lost in the Circuit Court. No fault of Dermot's.' *Thank you, Margaret.* 'But we must do better tomorrow. Tomorrow is the end of the road. Please tell me all there is to know about your unfortunate accident, in your own words, in your own time. There is no hurry. We are, as it were, *à votre service.* Isn't that so, Dermot?'

What was Margaret at? If she had nothing better to do that evening, I certainly had. All I wanted was to get out of that consultation as quickly as possible. There was much drafting to be done before dawn. 'Absolutely Margaret. All the time in the world. You have our exclusive attention, Professor, for as long as it takes,' I lied.

The professor needed no further encouragement. He was off.

The chimes of the grandfather clock came and went. Professor Moriarty went on and on, interrupted occasionally by a question from Margaret. I did my best to keep awake by focusing on the rugby photographs, still unable to confirm the professor's presence.

Eventually, things broke up. There wasn't a blade of Trinity's hallowed grass that we weren't familiar with by the time Margaret decided she had had enough. Presumably she had remembered an evening engagement. The salty one was long since gone when, at last, we followed suit. My night was in shreds.

*

We assembled in the Round Hall shortly after ten o'clock the following morning, and at ten thirty we went into Court 1 for the call-over of the list.

'I'll take the first case Moriarty *v.* Trinity College at eleven. As for the rest of the list, I have no more judges,' announced Ms Justice Doherty. 'The government keeps talking about new appointments but I'm afraid they won't be made today, so the other cases will just have to back-up. Hopefully, once you get your legendary negotiation skills working, many of the cases will settle.' With a smile, the jewel in the High Court crown rose from her seat overlooking her courtroom and followed her crier into her chambers for a well-earned cup of tea.

As the chattering court emptied into the Round Hall, Margaret took her opponent Sebastian Carroll, B.L. aside. I went with her. Sebastian had hockeyed me in the Circuit Court and perhaps that was why Trinity hadn't bothered with a Senior for the appeal.

'I'm happy we'll win this time,' Margaret said to Sebastian, 'but of course there are always risks.'

177

'What are you saying?' Sebastian asked impatiently. It was well known that Sebastian resented the fact that Margaret, though considerably junior to him, had taken silk and he hadn't.

'What I am saying, if you would allow me to finish, is that I am prepared to settle.'

'I am sure you are, Margaret. So would I be if I was in your position.'

'I will give you a discount, Sebastian. The case is worth twenty. Dermot tells me that previously there was an offer of ten. Put something on top of that and I will recommend it to my client,' Margaret continued, undaunted.

'You wouldn't like a share in Trinity as well, I suppose?' Sebastian replied.

'No, thank you. I am just trying to do the best for my client and, if in the process we can save some court time and get on to more lucrative pastures, so much the better.'

'Very noble, Margaret, except for one thing.'

'And what is that?'

'Liability.' Sebastian is known in the law library as a pedantic barrister.

'How so?' Margaret pretended she didn't know.

'"Cycling Prohibited",' he said. The sign had won him the case in the Circuit Court.

'I suppose we're going on then, Sebastian,' said Margaret. 'It's almost eleven. Do you want to take instructions?'

'I've already done so,' replied the doyen of pedants. 'The college is adamant. They believe they've treated your client fairly. He had his chance.'

'Well, in that case, let's get on with it,' Margaret urged as she turned on her heels and made for court.

'Just one matter, Margaret.'

'Yes, Sebastian.'

'Apparently Judge Doherty was a student of the plaintiff's some years ago.'

'So?'

'Well, my people are concerned that she may have a bias in favour of her old teacher.'

'Did she have an affair with him?'

'There is more to bias than sex, Margaret, as you well know.'

'As far as I can see that ball can bounce either way. She may love him, she may hate him. We'll have to take our chances.' Margaret didn't wait for Sebastian's response. She went into court and I followed.

The judge had presumably enjoyed a pleasant cup of tea and was back on the bench. 'Ms Thompson, Mr Carroll, I have had an opportunity to read the pleadings and I see that the case involves Professor Moriarty on the one hand and Trinity College on the other. Now, you may not know this but, first of all, I attended Trinity College and, secondly, I was a student of Professor Moriarty's. I think it only right that I should make this clear at the outset lest there be a concern afterwards. I assume that there is no objection to my hearing the case? Ms Thompson?'

'None, My Lord.'

'Mr Carroll?'

'Em ...'

'Yes, Mr Carroll?'

'Well, My Lord ...'

'Mr Carroll, if you have an objection, please say so.'

'Yes, My Lord.'

'You have an objection?'

'No, My Lord.'

'Well then, perhaps we can get on with the case,' the judicial jewel declared.

'But, Sebastian ...' Sebastian's solicitor whispered across the table, but it was too late.

In no time at all Margaret had opened our case to the court and Professor Moriarty, looking even more like Ken Dodd than he had in the Circuit Court, was settling himself in the witness box.

'It's nice to see you again after all these years, Professor,' the judge said, sounding like a chat-show host.

'And may I return the compliment, My Lord.'

'Ms Thompson will have a few questions for you.'

'Thank you, My Lord.'

'And of course we must not forget Mr Carroll. He will probably want to ask you a few questions also,' Doherty said with a smile in Sebastian's direction.

'Professor Moriarty, perhaps you would be good enough to tell Judge Doherty about your accident,' Margaret began.

'Of course, Ms Thompson ... from the beginning?' the Professor enquired.

'Oh, I don't think so, Professor. Her Lordship has read the pleadings and I have opened the case, so perhaps we could fast-forward to the accident itself.'

'I don't wish to influence how you examine your witness, Ms Thompson,' interrupted the Judge, 'but it might be better if Professor Moriarty were to start at the beginning.'

'Very well, My Lord.'

After his experience in the Circuit Court, the professor might have been forgiven for thinking he had wandered into a massage parlour, such was the warmth of his welcome. At this stage of the Circuit Court proceedings, Judge Pilkington had more or less informed the professor that his life to date had been a waste of time and that academia was full of people who couldn't make it in the real world.

Prompted by Margaret, the professor presented his case in an efficient and understated manner such that the judge could not but have been impressed had she needed impressing. At the end of his account, the case seemed a simple one. The wrong done to Professor Moriarty that Halloween howled for a remedy.

That was not how it seemed to Sebastian, who now rose to cross-examine. 'Professor, I have no wish to waste the valuable time of the court.' To be fair to Sebastian, he was dull but he didn't waste time. 'Nor indeed your valuable time. Therefore I will come to the point. May I refer you to the booklet of photographs we had in the Circuit Court and, in particular, number 11.' The photographs were handed to the professor and to the judge.

'I have photograph number 11,' said the professor.

'Please tell the court what it records.'

'We dealt with this in the Circuit Court, Mr Carroll. The writing on the sign – which is what you are getting at, I think – is not clear. However, it was agreed that it says "Cycling Prohibited".'

'Precisely.' Sebastian paused theatrically. '"Cycling Prohibited".' Sebastian was revving up. His foot was now up on the bench – full flight was not far away. 'And the words "Cycling Prohibited", do they convey anything in particular to you, Professor?'

'What they say, I suppose,' the professor answered sheepishly.

'Precisely,' Sebastian said in a self-congratulatory tone. 'In a nutshell, that is the defence, Professor – that you were cycling in an area where cycling was prohibited and that, consequently, your accident is not the responsibility of the university.' Sebastian must have felt that he couldn't put his case any more succinctly, and so he rested.

The professor must have been resting also for he said nothing. He stared at Sebastian and, when he tired of him, he stared at the judge. For his part, Sebastian stared down at his brief and for hers the judge stared at the top of Sebastian's head. All of this staring went on for some time until, eventually, Sebastian looked up from his brief and addressed the witness.

'Well?' he said.

'Well, what?' the witness replied.

'What is your answer to my question?' Sebastian explained.

'But that wasn't a question,' the professor protested, 'that was a statement.'

'Doesn't the plaintiff have a point, My Lord?' Margaret interrupted.

'Whether he does or he doesn't, Ms Thompson, what I would like to know from you, Mr Carroll, is this. I remember cycling in this very area of the college myself. Not today or yesterday, I admit. Do people still cycle there?'

'They do, My Lord,' replied Sebastian.

'Doesn't the fact that people still cycle there negative the prohibition?'

'I agree, My Lord,' Margaret added, out of turn.

'You will have your turn, Ms Thompson,' the judge said. 'Mr Carroll?'

'No, My Lord,' Sebastian replied. 'If we were dealing with a minor, I would have to agree with you. But we're not. We are dealing with an adult.' He looked over at the professor who was scratching his head.

'I see. Thank you, Mr Carroll. Please continue with your cross-examination.'

'I have no further questions for this witness, My Lord.' Sebastian sat down. The professor went back to his place.

Margaret called our next witness. 'Mr Hopkins, please tell Her Lordship your position in Trinity College.'

'I am the head porter, Judge.'

'And where is your office?'

'At the main gate under the Front Arch.'

'Were you there in the seventies, Mr Hopkins?' interrupted Doherty.

'I certainly was, Judge. And the sixties.'

'I remember you. You got on very well with the students,' Doherty said.

'Thank you, Judge. I like the students – and the professors. Indeed, I remember Professor Moriarty when he was a young lecturer.' The head porter smiled down at the professor. 'I don't remember you, Judge. Did you play hockey?'

'Not very well,' the judge replied. 'Now, Mr Hopkins, if you would answer Ms Thompson's questions.'

'Of course, Judge.' At this point, Sebastian must have been regretting his failure to object to Judge Doherty hearing the case.

'Please tell the court about cycling in the university,' Margaret said to the witness.

'It's quite simple really. Traditionally, walking and cycling were the two ways of getting around the college. You could cycle everywhere. Cars were banned.'

'Did that change, Mr Hopkins?'

'Unfortunately. A few years ago, the college authorities decided to allow cars in on a restricted basis and, to facilitate this, cycling was prohibited in certain areas.'

'Was the area where Professor Moriarty had his accident one of those areas?'

'It was.'

'What happened after the ban was introduced? Was it enforced?'

'It was. Indeed, my fellow porters and I were responsible for enforcing it.'

'And did you?'

'We did.'

'In all prohibited areas?'

'Not all, no.'

'Was there any reason for that?'

'Well, the ban wasn't popular with the students or the academics. So we were selective. Cars didn't bother with

183

a few of the prohibited areas and so we left them alone. Market forces as it were.'

'Did you enforce it in the area where the accident occurred?'

'No.'

'So, what happened there?'

'Cycling continued.'

'Thank you, Mr Hopkins. Please answer any questions my friend might have.'

'Mr Carroll, do you have a few questions for Mr Hopkins?' Judge Doherty asked Sebastian, adding a touch of judicial pressure to his task.

'I do, My Lord. I won't be long,' replied Sebastian.

'Take as long as you like, Mr Carroll.'

'Mr Hopkins, you have had a long career in the porters' office in Trinity, is that so?' Sebastian asked.

'I have been fortunate, Mr Carroll.'

'And, as my friend has said, you have enjoyed popularity among students and staff alike?'

'It's nice of you to say so. I've done my best.'

'Moving to the facts of the case, Mr Hopkins, I think it's well known that you were never a fan of the cycling ban, isn't that so?'

'My views were well known. I didn't make a secret of them.'

'I am instructed that the ban was somewhat controversial when it was introduced. Is that correct?'

'It is.'

'And there were a number of protests?'

'There were – from students and staff.'

'So it's fair to say, I think, that no one studying or working in the university could have been unaware of its introduction?'

'Yes.'

'The court can take it then that Professor Moriarty must have known that cycling was prohibited?'

Margaret tried to object.

'I can't answer for the professor but the ban did receive a lot of publicity at the time.'

'Mr Hopkins, you have told the court that, in the area where the professor had his accident, cycling continued after the prohibition was introduced, isn't that so?'

'It is.'

'Whether or not that is relevant is a matter for Her Lordship.' Sebastian looked up at Judge Doherty. 'But one thing is certain. At the time of this accident, the byelaws of the university prohibited cycling in this area, is that not so?'

Mr Hopkins hesitated. Sebastian repeated his question.

'It is,' Mr Hopkins answered. Sebastian sat down.

'Thank you, Mr Hopkins, you are ...' the judge began.

'Before Your Lordship releases Mr Hopkins, I have one or two questions arising from cross-examination,' Margaret said.

'Of course, Ms Thompson.'

'Mr Hopkins, you seemed to hesitate when Mr Carroll referred to the byelaws of the university. Why was that?'

'I'm not a lawyer, Ms Thompson.'

'No harm in that,' interjected Doherty.

'But I couldn't find a record of the decision to prohibit cycling when I went looking for it,' Mr Hopkins continued.

Margaret was puzzled. 'Why were you looking for a record of the decision?'

'You'd know more about these things, Ms Thompson, being a barrister. All I know is that the first thing I was shown all those years ago when I started as a junior porter was this big ledger containing the byelaws of the college. I was told that it was very important and to take care of it.'

That was the first we'd heard of this.

'Why was it so important?' Margaret asked.

'I was told that under the college charter all decisions grounding byelaws had to be recorded in this ledger.'

Judge Doherty was interested. 'So, if a decision is made by the college authorities but not recorded it means that there is no decision. Is that what you are saying, Mr Hopkins?'

'I'm only telling you what I was told, Judge.'

'And you checked the register and couldn't find the decision. Is that right?' the judge continued.

'For certain, Judge. I checked and rechecked. No decision.'

Margaret, beaming, turned around to me.

'Excuse me for interrupting, Ms Thompson,' said the judge.

'Not at all, My Lord. Most helpful,' Margaret replied.

Doherty turned to Sebastian. 'Mr Carroll, what do you say about all this. Isn't it the final nail in your coffin, as it were?'

'Certainly not, My Lord. What Mr Hopkins is talking about is merely housekeeping.'

'But it's your charter, Mr Carroll, and it says that decisions must be recorded.'

'I submit not, My Lord. The sign is there for all to see. Everyone knows that cycling is prohibited. The professor ignores the sign at his peril. The rest is housekeeping.'

'I don't agree, Mr Carroll. In fact, I think I've heard enough.'

'But, My Lord ...' Sebastian tried to rein in the judge, but she was not to be stopped.

'No, Mr Carroll, my mind is made up. From the outset, I had a hunch about this case. The more I heard, the more satisfied I became. Indeed, I think that the defendant cannot be proud of how it has treated its distinguished servant in relation to his claim. No fault of yours,

Mr Carroll. You have your instructions. The plaintiff succeeds. I have read the medical reports and it seems to me that the injuries warrant the full jurisdiction. Therefore, judgment for £30,000. Thank you both.'

'May it please Your Lordship,' Margaret said quietly.

'Costs, Margaret,' Arnold prompted, as if she might forget.

'Costs in both courts, Ms Thompson,' Judge Doherty said, as if she had heard. She smiled at her former teacher as he left the room. The next case was called.

In the corridor there were scenes of jubilation. The professor had a big hug for Margaret and Samantha and looked as if he was heading for me. I extended my hand quickly and he shook it warmly.

He said that he would definitely buy a new bicycle. Samantha warned him about potted plants. Arnold thought Margaret had done a wonderful job and 'how Pilkington got it so wrong in the Circuit Court' he would never know. 'Mac, your Opinion was right after all,' he said to me. 'I never doubted you.'

The professor said he would like to thank Judge Doherty in person and made for her chambers. Margaret cut him off, explaining that she was still sitting.

Another *pro bono* brought home. What would Rachel say now?

COURT 1

Deep in West Cork there is a tennis club of which my dear aunt is a member. My aunt is a protestant and indeed has been for some time. Tennis has been played there since around the time Jane Austen first set eyes on the young barrister later to become chief justice of Ireland. Many of the club's traditions continue to this day.

At the fourth chime of the church clock on sunny afternoons between May and September, the tea hostess sounds a gong. Instantly, the courts – grass only – clear and the players – in whites only – make their way to the corrugated pavilion for tea and crustless cucumber sandwiches.

Deep in Dublin 4 there is another tennis club, a sister to my aunt's club in West Cork. Both clubs share a protestant heritage, an insistence on whites and a tranquillity that, while not unexpected in West Cork, comes as a surprise behind the petrol station in Donnybrook. In recent times, the grass courts in Donnybrook Lawn Tennis Club have disappeared, and of course the tea hostess only exists in the black and white photographs that adorn the walls of the pavilion.

More recently, enthusiastic presidents have sought to drag this jewel of clubs into modern times. At a modest level, the introduction of croissants and newspapers has boosted buzz and revenue at weekends. More alarmingly, there have been rumours of underground parking and a high-rise pavilion. Even a change of address has been

189

mentioned. To date, these ambitions have been resisted by a discerning membership that puts the pastoral integrity of the club before progress. Anyone who has ever watched the sun go down on these courts as the last points of a summer evening are played will appreciate the wisdom of the members.

*

The thirty-first of July is the high watermark of legal celebration. On that day the doors of the Law Library close forever, or at least until October, which is about as close as a barrister is likely to get to eternity. June and July go on forever. Tempers and temperatures soar. It may not be Delhi but the sun shines, it becomes humid and the heating remains on. Occasionally, a sympathetic judge invites counsel to remove their wigs as a concession to the season.

After long days in court, at night there is the vain attempt to clear the backlog of paperwork. Enquiries from panicking solicitors, fearful that the courts may not re-open, test the equanimity of even the most unflappable barrister. Twenty-four-hour days. Seven-day weeks. One last effort in the dying moments of the legal year.

The respective clubs and societies within the Library compete with one another for the few hours that members might take off to avert a breakdown. The Golf Society travels to Baltray for Captain's Prize and then a summer party in Mount Juliet. Traditionally, the last Sunday in July is reserved for tennis. The Bar hosts the annual match against the Bench at Donnybrook Lawn Tennis Club.

With Afric in charge of Bar and Mr Justice Fleming in charge of Bench, the annual encounter is a competitive one, approached on both sides in a friendly spirit. In the past, the fixture was more evenly balanced, the trophy changing hands most years. Recently, a rising Bar and an ageing Bench had resulted in a six-year-on-the-trot deficit for Fleming and his judicial cohorts.

Towards the middle of July, rumour reached the Library that Fleming was intent on reversing this trend. He had selected his squad earlier than usual and they were in training. Off the booze, in bed early and no heavy cases. Fitzwilliam Tennis Club's facilities were stretched to their limit as Fleming and his team prepared. While selection was not a problem as the pool of players was small, two recent appointments to the Bench meant that the average age of the judges' team was reduced by ten years. Fleming and his colleagues meant business.

Afric's problems were different. Demand greatly exceeded supply. The fixture was a popular one in the Library and anyone who could hold a racquet wanted to be on the team. In truth, like the All Blacks, Afric could field two first teams and perhaps three. They might not all win the World Cup but would certainly test the best the Bench could offer. While she was always keen to win, she decided that, this year, the emphasis should be on the Corinthian spirit. The task of selection was approached accordingly. After all, another win would not make future appearances in court any easier.

Afric's team went up on the pillar in the Law Library on the Monday before the match. There were those who were disappointed and those who were pleasantly surprised. Some of the women were chosen for their looks, some of the men because no combination of circumstances or conditions could result in them winning their matches. Afric didn't tell me, but I suspected that this was the category into which I fell. Victory now was an unlikely eventuality and, from Afric's point of view, the day was already a success.

The great day dawned. Sun poured down from a cloudless heaven and, on the dot of eleven, I jumped out of bed full of the joys of vacation. This was one of the few opportunities for a family get-together enjoyed by the Bar and so, while I assembled my kit, Rachel assembled the kids and *en famille* we made our way to this tennis oasis in the heart of Dublin 4.

On the dot of two, a host of cloudless barristers and judges descended upon Donnybrook LTC. The club never looked so well. It sparkled like a diamond sea on this last afternoon of July as the players warmed up on the courts that stretch as far as the monastic wall that separates the club from the convent beside it. The trophy, as fine as the Sam Maguire itself, was presented by a former chief justice many decades earlier. Having adorned the shelves of the Law Library for the previous six years, it calmly awaited its fate. Would it return to the Library or would it, as Mr Justice Fleming earnestly hoped, make its way to a new home in his chambers? The polished trophy gave no clue as to its preference. It simply rested there waiting to be claimed.

As captain of the host team, Afric was in charge and, as a member of Donnybrook Tennis Club, she was on home ground. Like a politician at election time, she was in her element. Everyone was given a warm welcome, especially the captain of the judges, Fleming, J. He was partial to a female partner and so chose Ms Justice Doherty to play with. A trifle *feminista* for our Fleming, she was however an accomplished player and togged out well. Unfortunately, she arrived with a touch of tennis elbow and had to withdraw. Fleming sought Afric's inspiration. The other female judges were spoken for and so would it be possible for him to borrow one of Afric's reserves? Afric rose to the occasion. Margaret Thompson, S.C., of course. Fleming was delighted.

By one of those charming coincidences that illuminate life, who did I see parking his bicycle in the space reserved for the president of the club, but Professor Moriarty of Tour de Trinity fame. He shook my hand warmly and welcomed me to his club, embraced Margaret and almost smothered Judge Doherty in his attempt to thank her for her decision on his appeal.

Shortly after he arrived, the professor, who might have been more at home with croquet than tennis, rang the bell to signal the formal announcement of the teams. All assembled in the colourful garden in front of the clubhouse. The players were resplendent in their snow-white tennis gear. With one exception. The captain himself, Judge Fleming, was wearing a tennis shirt the colour of which was closer to Van Gogh's sunflowers than the dress code of Donnybrook LTC.

Fleming, oblivious to the tension that he was responsible for stirring in the heart of the professor, was making his way to the centre of the gathering to announce his selection. The professor, a copy of the club rules under his arm, was moving to head him off. Margaret, alert, had a word in Judge Doherty's ear. Doherty was on her feet immediately, just in time to intercept the professor before he tapped Fleming on the shoulder with the rules. She whisked the professor into the clubhouse where she ordered two gin and tonics.

Fleming, still oblivious, was on his feet addressing the courtside crowd. The announcement of each of his pairings was greeted with hoots of approval and applause. The greatest hoot of approval was reserved for the announcement of his final pairing, Margaret and himself.

'May the best team win,' he concluded.

Afric followed with her pairings. More hoots. More applause.

'Let the games begin!' the professor shouted from the bar, a gin and tonic in one hand and Judge Doherty in the other. Fleming's Van Gogh was forgotten.

The six matches made their way to their respective courts. The flagship match for the first half of the afternoon was sent to Court 1. Mr Justice Humphries of the High Court and Judge Rogers of the Circuit Court faced Henry Fitzmartin, S.C. and Helen Davidson, B.L. The crowd focused on this match and from time to time Fleming and Afric brought news from the outlying courts of how the other matches were going.

Helen, finishing her devilling year, was in august company. Partnering the leader of our European Bar and opposing High and Circuit Court judges, it was no wonder she was nervous. It would have been nice if she had had accomplishment as a tennis player to fall back on, but it was clear from early on that this was not part of the package.

It doesn't necessarily follow that, if one is an unexciting barrister, one will be an unexciting tennis player. It's just that very often it turns out that way. As it did with Henry. A courteous partner for Helen he may have been, an exciting tennis player for those watching he was not. It was no surprise that the backbone of his game was the 'Garryowen'. 'Up to Holy God!' roared the crowd every time he launched another lob.

Afric and I had played before with Rogers in the President's Prize in Milltown. A low handicapper, his golf was like his judging: straight down the middle, no time wasted, no frills. His tennis was like his golf but not as good. He suffered from a low boredom threshold and from time to time this interfered with what he was trying to achieve with the tennis ball.

Humphries, J. is something of a contradiction. His court is a centre of truth. He has a razor sharp mind and a razor sharp backhand, but the cornerstone of his game was his bad calls.

'In' and 'out' are two words that are as old as the English language itself. Historically, they are simple words with nothing pretentious about them. They are not given to ambiguity and mean what they say. Until the game of tennis came along, they had a low profile and did not court controversy. The rules of tennis provide that, if a ball is inside the line, it is 'in', outside the line, it is 'out' and, crucially, if it is on the line, it is 'in'. Could anything be simpler?

Most tennis matches do not come with an umpire and so the players are called upon to make their own decisions as to whether a ball is 'in' or 'out'. The correctness of these decisions depends on the eyesight of the player calling and his integrity. Nobody for a moment doubted either the eyesight or the integrity of Humphries. And yet, from time to time, a ball that seemed to the spectators to land 'on the line' in Humphries' corner of the court, and therefore seemed to be 'in', was called 'out', and a ball that seemed to the spectators to land 'outside the line' on his opponents' side of the net, and therefore seemed to be 'out', was called 'in'. These complexities arose most often on points that mattered.

One couldn't judge Rogers for not raising Judge Humphries' calls as an issue. He was, after all, Humphries' partner. Clearly, it wasn't a matter for Helen. It was up to Henry who, to the delight of the crowd, had no compunctions about questioning them. At this stage of his career he didn't have to bother too much about ruffling judicial feathers and, in any event, his court appearances were mainly in Europe.

Every time Helen came within an ass's roar of the ball, the crowd got behind her. She looked about fifteen and was as pretty as a rose. Most of the time she failed to make contact but, when she did, her opponents were so taken by surprise that her shot proved to be a winner and the crowd went wild.

Henry's lobs were not always successful, but every time they were launched the crowd got behind them too. There was a reasonable chance that the response would end up in the net, particularly if Rogers was on the other end.

The judges won the first set comfortably but Henry managed to keep his team in touch in the second. The lobs were beginning to get to Rogers, who had never regarded them as an acceptable feature of the game of tennis.

It was six-five to Helen and Henry in the tie-break in the second set. Set point. Miraculously, Helen connected. The crowd roared. Not a winner this time but the ball went down Humphries' tramlines. He hit a wonderful backhand to Henry who calmly launched the highest lob of the match so far. The crowd roared again.

All eyes were on Rogers who was assembling himself below. This smash for six all. The ball was taking forever to descend. Rogers waited. The ball arrived at last. Rogers let go. But no. The ball was in the net. Half an inch higher and it would have been the smash of the match. Second set to the Bar. One set all.

Rogers let go again, 'For God's sake Henry, can you do nothing else?' The crowd erupted.

From time to time, the two captains visited the suburban courts and returned with news of the other matches. It was nip and tuck. Two matches were favouring the judges, one the Bar. The other two were too close to call.

This one was now in the third set. The sun poured down. Helen was playing out of her skin. Winners were coming from her racquet fast and furious. How, no one knew. Henry was having even more success with his lobs and Rogers was crumbling. The judges would have to depend on Humphries' razor sharp backhand and, of course, his bad calls, which were increasing exponentially.

Word filtered through from the other courts. The Bench had won three matches, the Bar two. This was no longer a friendly. Helen and Henry had to win to keep the afternoon alive.

'Good shot, Judge,' Ronald Browning shouted, announcing his late arrival. Humphries had just hit a magnificent volley, giving Henry no chance. In fairness, Helen and Henry were giving it their all. Humphries and Rogers had been odds-on favourites. But Henry's lobs had well and truly got to Rogers so that he wasn't really in the frame. More and more, Humphries was taking control of his side of the net.

It was forty-thirty on Humphries' serve and three all. The vital seventh game. He wouldn't normally serve hard to his female opponent, but this was no time for chivalry. Helen was playing too well and so he cut loose with a huge serve, which only a matter of games earlier she would not have seen let alone returned. But now back it went, straight down Rogers' tramlines, giving him no chance. It was clearly, unambiguously in. But not to Humphries. 'Out!' he called. Henry was furious and glared at Humphries. 'Good call, Judge!' was heard from an anonymous source in the crowd that Humphries tried unsuccessfully to locate. The score was four-three to the judges.

Somehow Helen held her serve and Rogers lost his so that, against the odds, Henry was serving for the match. Forty-thirty. Second serve. Served softly to be safe. Into Rogers' backhand. Nervously returned. To Henry. Up to Holy God. Where else? More to the back of the court than he would have liked. Humphries waiting. The ball landed. On the line. In the corner. Not an inch to spare.

'Out!' Humphries called.

'In!' roared the crowd. He had no choice but to play it back to his opponents. The ball was more Henry's side but Helen suddenly appeared from nowhere. At the net. Poaching. In total control. A player transformed. She hit the ball in the middle of her racquet and put it away.

Rogers was never going to get to it. The pairings shook hands. Three matches all. One to go. The convent bell struck four. The professor, another gin and tonic in one hand and the afternoon tea bell in the other, announced the interval. And the sun poured down.

Players and spectators filled the pavilion and the garden outside. There was quite a buzz. Between the weather and vacation and now the closeness of the match, there was plenty to be excited about.

John, Donnybrook's maître d', allows himself to be seconded once a year to indulge the culinary weaknesses of Bar and Bench. Once again, he had surpassed himself. With his *crème de* this and *crème de* that, the pavilion looked like a patisserie from a Parisian high street.

Ronald Browning asked Judge Doherty if she would care for a *Millefeuille á la framboise*. Ronald is not a tennis player but neither is he one to miss an opportunity to cultivate the Bench. His tour of the pavilion had begun, as had mine as I helped Afric with the afternoon tea.

'Thank you, Ronald,' said Doherty. 'I must say John puts on a great show every year. I always look forward to it.'

'I wouldn't miss it for the world.' Ronald was looking closely at Doherty. 'You're not togged out, Judge? Aren't you playing with Judge Fleming?'

'I was supposed to be but I have a touch of tennis elbow. Didn't think you could get it playing at my level. Unfortunately, I've had to pull out.'

'Oh, that's too bad. He's disappointed, I'm sure.'

'I think he's over his disappointment,' Doherty said, pointing to a table overlooking the courts where Fleming was helping Margaret to her strawberries. 'Afric gave him Margaret Thompson in my place.'

'I see what you mean,' Ronald replied, looking over. He moved on.

'Bad luck, Judge,' he said to Humphries, adding, after he had satisfied himself that Rogers was not in earshot, 'not your fault.'

'Oh it's not a question of fault, Ronald. It's only a game, after all. You're right though. Rogers was not at his best. And then some of the calls didn't go our way.' I wondered which particular calls he had in mind.

'I was just saying that to Judge Doherty. Anyway it makes for an exciting finale.'

Ronald spotted Rogers nearby and, leaving Humphries, shuffled towards him. 'Bad luck with your match, Judge. Henry does overdo the lobs.'

'Well, if that isn't the understatement of the year. Can he do anything else?' Rogers hadn't yet come to terms with the result.

'I don't know how you kept your cool. He would test the patience of a saint.'

'I'm not sure that I did, Ronald. At one point I lost it a bit.'

'Not at all. You were quite right to let him have it just that once. Anyway, it was a great match and there's another one to go.' Again, Ronald moved on. Perhaps the chief justice had arrived.

Fleming moved into the bar to get a medicinal gin and tonic before going on court. To calm the nerves, you know. Margaret went with him. They were deep in discussion. Tactics, perhaps. They were interrupted by the arrival of Laurence with the wine list.

'Everyone says you're the favourites,' Laurence announced to the two of them.

'I hope not. We'd much prefer to be the underdogs,' Fleming replied.

'Well, on any assessment, Mac isn't up to much and, unless his tennis is a big improvement on his golf, you should win in straight sets.' There were disadvantages to helping with the afternoon tea. I pretended not to hear.

'Afric is a superb tennis player,' Margaret chipped in magnanimously. 'And anyway, Laurence, you know what they say about counting your chickens.'

Laurence wasn't a bit interested in chickens and instead turned his attention to John behind the bar. Fleming and Margaret resumed their tactics.

'Have you no French wines?' Laurence enquired.

'I'm afraid not,' John replied. 'The members prefer the New World.'

'I'm not surprised. Why we don't hold this fixture in Fitzwilliam, I'll never understand.' While the absence of French wine was a disappointment to Laurence, it was not a deterrent and he ordered a glass of plonk from the New World.

Ronald joined Laurence briefly. He isn't one to waste time on his colleagues – the male ones anyway. 'Who is that talking to Henry?' Ronald whispered.

'That's Henry's partner.'

'I know that. I was watching the match. What's her name?'

'Helen Davidson. She's not long in,' Laurence replied, as if referring to some secret society.

'Gorgeous, isn't she? Poor thing having to put up with Henry. I'd better go and rescue her.'

Not knowing Helen, Ronald addressed Henry. 'Well done, Henry. Great match. You certainly put the judges in their place. As for Humphries' calls. Unbelievable. The integrity of the Bench, how are you.' Turning towards Henry's gorgeous partner, he said, 'Helen, I don't think we've met. I'm Ronald Browning, North Western Circuit.'

'Hello, Ronald. Were you watching our match?'

'I most certainly was, Helen. You play a good game.'

'Oh, I don't. It was all thanks to Henry. The judges couldn't handle his lobs.'

'I don't blame them for that. But your winning shot was a beauty. They couldn't get near it. You obviously play quite a lot.'

'You're saying all the right things. Unfortunately I don't, but maybe it's not too late to start.'

The professor was ringing his bell for all he was worth. He seemed to be enjoying the afternoon thoroughly. Clearly he loved showing off his club. The interval was over and it was time for the showdown. The professor did his best, bearing in mind his condition, to announce the final pairings. What he said was utterly unintelligible but it didn't matter. It was merely a touch of old-fashioned pomp and ceremony. Everyone knew the pairings, even the pairings themselves. Afric had invited him to umpire the final match and so he made his way to the umpire's chair. He could hardly walk. For the second time that afternoon, Doherty intercepted him and dragged him back to the bar. At short notice, a substitute assumed the umpire's seat.

Fleming led Margaret and Afric led me onto the show court to excited applause. Fifty or so giddy spectators lined the court. Every deckchair was occupied and every blade of grass. Tans were exposed and much else. The match was level and so the winner of our game would lift the trophy. There was everything to play for.

I hadn't been so nervous since my golf debut with Afric in Milltown for the President's Prize. I had been told that my tennis was better than my golf, but there wasn't much in it and I wasn't used to an audience. As early as the knock-up it was clear that our opponents had identified me as the weak link. More than likely, they had worked this out before coming on court, but during the knock-up it was obvious that they were going to play me. A torrid afternoon lay ahead.

As host captain, Afric tossed. Fleming, visiting captain, called. Afric to serve. The girls removed their tracksuits. The Bench was playing from south to north. Afric serving with her back to the city. No wind. Not a cloud in the sky. Conditions perfect. 'Good luck,' she wished the Bench.

'Good luck,' Fleming wished us back.

Love all. Play. Afric, tall and thin and tanned, looked magnificent as she threw up the ball as a prelude to the first serve of the match. As a matter of factual accuracy, I assumed rather than knew that she looked magnificent. At that moment, as her partner, I was of course at the net adopting an upside down 'L' position and couldn't actually see her. I was doing my best to replicate what I had seen them do at Wimbledon over the years. Her serve whizzed past my right ear at 100 miles per hour to Fleming's backhand.

Fleming is an elegant player if, at this point in his career, a little portly. He likes to tell anyone who will listen about playing for Ireland in the Davis Cup. It isn't clear whether it was in his twenties or the twenties. No one doubts that he did in fact represent his country. It is just that there is no independent evidence. So far, attempts to track down a witness or a record have been unsuccessful.

Even a former Davis Cup player is entitled to a weakness in his game and Afric had identified it in the warm-up. Now, on the first point of the match, she was letting Fleming know that she knew about his backhand – or the lack of it. He did what he always did in such circumstances – ran around it. In doing so, he collided with Margaret who liked to play on the baseline and, in the course of all this, put the ball into the net. Fifteen-love. Afric had got us off to a good start.

I crossed court to face Margaret, who seemed delighted to be teamed up with Fleming and to be the centre of attention on this tennis occasion. Standing on the baseline, shifting her weight from one foot to another, I could see that Afric's serve had her full attention. Once again, Afric lofted her ball and unleashed. This time it went past my left ear on to Margaret's backhand.

Margaret did not play Davis Cup tennis but she did have a backhand and she unwound mercilessly. I was sure that I was covering my trams and that I would be able to pop the ball back. Unfortunately, the court was slightly wider than I was used to and so Margaret's backhand passed me. I couldn't lay a string on it and, inch perfect, it landed on the outside line, half-way between service and baseline.

'Oh my goodness, Virginia ... what a backhand,' I seemed to hear Wimbledon's Dan Maskell say.

'Brilliant,' Fleming shouted, 'brilliant!'

The crowd broke into spontaneous applause. 'That's my girl!' roared the professor from the bar. Fleming and Margaret celebrated with a high five and Afric consoled me. Not the start I needed.

Afric took full advantage of Fleming's backhand to win the opening game for us. It was our turn to face the relentless sun. Margaret had no difficulty winning her service game. One all, going with serve.

Service had never been the bedrock of my game. Indeed, my game didn't have a bedrock in any identifiable sense. My game plan was to reel from point to point, hoping for the best and that it would soon be over. If I could have got out of serving, I would have, but the rules didn't provide such an option. I took two balls and began bouncing one of them on the baseline as the top players do. When Afric looked around from her position at the net, I took this to be my cue to get on with it. Time to serve.

I threw the ball high in the air, making no allowance for the fact that there was no eclipse of the sun scheduled for that moment, with the result that I was completely blinded. There I was in front of the gallery, the ball in the air for my first serve, but with no idea as to its precise position. What could I do but go through the motions of serving and, in the pattern of my game, hope for the best? I let go with the racquet and waited for the connection. There wasn't any. Instead, the ball bounced off my forehead and onto the ground. The gallery thought it was great fun.

'*Oh dearie me,*' Dan said.

I repeated the procedure, this time making the connection. Double fault. Love-fifteen. A second double fault helped Fleming and Margaret to another game.

'Fleming and Margaret lead by two games to one,' the umpire announced as we changed ends. Much of Afric's concentration was going into consoling me. Fleming made it three-one and, in no time at all, with the assistance of another brace of double faults on my second service game, we were down the first set. 'First set to Fleming and Thompson by six games to two,' said the umpire.

'Good on you, Margaret!' the professor shouted through his gin and tonics when he heard the score.

'*Is there any way back for Afric and McNamara?*' Dan enquired of Virginia. Either Virginia didn't hear him or she didn't know because she certainly didn't answer.

We weren't due a change of ends but we took a little break anyhow. Fleming and Margaret were in great form basking in their lead. 'Only two service breaks in it,'

Margaret declared, meaning to be encouraging. These were mine unfortunately.

I apologised to Afric for letting her down. 'Don't be a silly,' she replied. 'It won't be any harm at all if the judges win.'

Going back on court, Fleming predicted that 'the opera ain't over till the fat lady sings.' What that had to do with us being one set down, I didn't know. Unfortunately, I had to serve the first game of the second set. Again into the sun. I had to do *something*. Maybe I wasn't any good at tennis, but I wasn't that bad. The occasion had got to me.

'Why don't you try the net, Dermot?' Afric suggested. The very thing, even if at that moment I was wondering if I wasn't a little out of my depth.

I borrowed a visor from the sideline, threw the ball sunwards and, before there was time to be blinded, served it with every ounce I could call on. It worked. Connection. The ball flew in Fleming's direction, this time in. Fleming was astonished. As was I. It even went down his backhand and he obliged by putting it into the net. The crowd took a moment to realise what had happened. It was fifteen-love. Margaret didn't do any better on my next serve. Perhaps a little complacency had settled on the favourites.

I was serving to Fleming for the second time in the second set. I bounced the ball. Up in the air. Followed through. Again, down his backhand. How, I had no idea. Fleming was ready this time. '*A perfect cross-court return from Fleming's backhand*,' commented Dan. But Fleming hadn't reckoned on the implementation of Afric's advice. I followed my serve to the net, swapping a serve-and-hope game for a game of serve and volley. I'd seen them do it often on the telly.

As I ran in, I stuck my racquet out, more in hope than confidence. By pure chance, as soon as the ball crossed the net, there was my racquet waiting for it. Without any input from me, the ball made contact with the centre of my outstretched racquet and re-crossed the net, making for Margaret's trams. Such was the speed at which things were happening on this point, and the surprise that I was in the thick of it, that Margaret had no chance. All she could do was helplessly watch the ball go past her. The crowd was on its feet. Afric gave me a high five. Fleming shouted, 'Well done, Dermot!'

'*My goodness, Virginia,*' Dan said.

We went on to win that game. Still, it was only one game and the score was far from level. There were no easy points. Fleming and Margaret were on their game and not making mistakes. Also, Fleming had begun to leave the shots down his backhand to his partner.

Forty-thirty, three all. Fleming served to me. He served wide. I barely got to it. The tip of my racquet just about put the ball back to Fleming. An unintentional lob towards the back of the court. Fleming was under it and made no mistake about putting it down the middle. Fleming didn't miss these.

'Good shot, Judge!' shouted Ronald, who didn't miss them either.

'Fleming and Margaret lead by four games to three in the second set, having won the first,' the umpire announced, a reminder that things were hotting up, if a reminder was needed. Any slip by us now and the judges were home.

'Come on, Dermot, let's bring it to a third,' Afric exhorted as we changed ends.

'Come on, Dad!' shouted Conor and Kate from the crowd.

With the exception of the professor and Doherty, still ensconced in their gin and tonics, everyone was focused on the match. Even Ronald, who was standing beside

Judge Humphries waiting for more 'good shots' from Judge Fleming.

The crowd, the majority of whom were barristers, willed us through the next three games and the second set.

'One set all,' said the umpire.

'*A turn-up for the books, Virginia. Isn't that what it's all about?*' Dan said. '*Tennis at its purest, the amateur game.*'

Deliberately, we took a little extra time over our end-change. For the moment, the advantage was with us. It was after five o'clock but the sun was not letting up. Nor were our opponents. The match was being played at quite a pace and had to take its toll on Fleming soon. There hadn't been an encounter like it for years.

Margaret opened the third set, which went with serve to four all. Then she, who had been so consistent all afternoon, faltered and it was five-four to us. It was my service and my chance for glory. An hour earlier everyone would have expected Fleming and Margaret to break back immediately. But my game had improved beyond recognition and even I half expected to serve out. Unfortunately, the nerves re-grouped in numbers. Two double faults. Love-thirty. A moment later, five all. Then six all. Tie-break.

The spectators were vociferous. Even the judges, usually more reserved, were roused. 'Come on Fleming!' Humphries shouted. 'Let's see you.' Whatever that meant.

I served first. Down Fleming's forehand for a change. Back to Afric. Cross court to Margaret. Back to my forehand. To Fleming. A strong ball to the back of the court. Was it too big?

'Out!' shouted Humphries, who had no business calling.

'On the line is in!' shouted the anonymous source.

'The ball was in,' said Fleming.

'McNamara, one-love,' ruled the umpire.

'*How sporting,*' said Dan.

Tie-break going with serve. Five all. Fleming to me. Out wide. His favourite. I got to it, just about. I lobbed Margaret. Fleming would have got to it earlier in the afternoon.

'Six-five to the Bar,' declared the umpire. 'Match point.'

Afric served to Margaret. Down the middle. Margaret to me at the net. Back to Fleming on the baseline. Fleming in trouble. Scrambled it skywards. Middle of the court. 'Mine!' I shouted. Earlier I would have left it to Afric. The crowd roared. I prepared. The crowd went silent again. Not a word from Dan. The sun was in my eyes. The ball arrived. I let it bounce. Up it rose again. I pounced. My racquet was over my head. I let go. I knew the moment I connected. The ball went deep into Margaret's corner, giving her no chance.

'Game, set and match to Afric and McNamara, two-six, six-four, seven-five in the tie-break,' came the umpire's final announcement.

The crowd was on its feet. Afric and I embraced. 'Well done, Dermot,' she said, with a big kiss. 'We weren't supposed to win, you know.'

'That's why I was picked I suppose?'

'Well ...' She couldn't finish whatever it was she wanted to say as it was time to shake hands with Margaret and Fleming. The fans gave us a standing ovation.

'I was sure it was our turn this year,' Fleming said across the net.

'So was I,' said Afric, smiling.

'There's always next year,' temporary Judge Margaret chipped in.

'*Funny old game tennis, Virginia,*' said Dan as we left court.

Everyone, even the professor, gathered in the garden outside the pavilion.

'I would like to call on the president of Donnybrook Lawn Tennis Club to say a few words and present the trophy,' Afric said, in her capacity as host captain.

Professor Moriarty stepped forward in a circuitous manner. God knows how many gin and tonics he'd had at this stage. Certainly, the bicycle would be staying behind at the end of the day. 'Thank you very much, Afric. First of all, I would like to congratulate my favourite student, who is also my favourite judge, on her superlative judgment in my recent appeal,' the professor began, surprisingly coherent but clearly no longer with the plot.

Doherty was slow off the mark, partly because of her own alcohol intake presumably, but also because she was busy propping up the professor. 'The tennis, Professor, don't mind the judgment,' she prompted at last.

'Oh yes, the tennis … what about the tennis?'

'Afric and Dermot … the winners … the trophy, Professor … present the trophy.'

'Of course, the trophy. Well, it's my pleasure as president of Donnybrook Lawn Tennis Club to present the trophy to the winners … em …'

'Afric and Dermot,' Doherty whispered loudly.

'Of course, Afric and Dermot. Congratulations to you both.' The professor, swaying, shook my hand warmly and gave Afric a big hug.

Afric raised the cup in the manner of champions and proceeded briefly to thank all involved, including Professor Moriarty for taking such a close interest in the bar, if not the tennis.

'Before we finish.' The professor was making a comeback. 'I have one final presentation.' What on earth could it be? 'Margaret and Judge Fleming put up a valiant

fight and I would like to present each of them, especially
Judge Fleming, with a Donnybrook tennis shirt.'

'Well done, Professor!' the crowd shouted.

The formalities were over. It was time to relax and enjoy
the afterglow.

'I didn't know you were so good at tennis, Dermot,' said
Rachel, giving me a warm kiss on both cheeks. Kate and
Conor were basking in my reflected glory for a change.

'Nor did I,' I replied.

'Bit of a dark horse, Mac,' said Fleming. 'I was really
keen to win this year. Well played.'

'Thanks, Judge. A bit more training yourself and you'll
be back on the Davis Cup team.'

'Oh no, I'm afraid that's history, Mac. As for you,
Rachel, do you remember the advice I gave you last
October?'

'Last October, Judge?'

'About taking silk.'

'Oh yes, of course I remember.'

'Well, I was serious. Now's the time. This October. Go
for it. What do you think, Mac?'

'Great idea, Judge.'

'I'll give it good thought during the vacation,' Rachel
said, delighted with Fleming's encouragement.

'Glass of wine, Rachel?' I asked.

'I'd love one, Dermot.'

'Afric?'

'Yes, please.'

We were sitting in the garden, looking out on the now
empty courts.

'Fleming has been saying I should take silk, Afric. What
do you think?' Rachel said.

'He's right, Rachel. You're certainly ready for it, and now
that Maeve has gone to the Bench there is an opening.'

'Dermot?'

'Yes, darling?'

'Silk, Dermot?'

'Who? Me?'

'No, not you. What Fleming was saying about me.'

'Sorry. I was thinking about the match. Fleming is always right, darling.'

'No seriously, Dermot.'

'Well, Rachel, we've plenty of time to discuss it. In the meantime – cheers, Afric, and well done on another victory. Cheers, Rachel, and good luck with your decision.'

Clinking glasses, we settled back in our deckchairs, savouring the moment. In a few hours, the sun would go down behind the convent wall.